Vivian's breath seized in her chest from the sheer sincerity she witnessed in Alonso's eyes. Swallowing hard, she did her best to retain some semblance of control.

"You're afraid," he continued. "You're afraid of this thing we have going on." He cradled her face between his hands. "This wild, insane, all-consuming energy we generate. You don't trust it. You don't trust it because you don't trust me. But that's okay. You will."

"Always the businessman. Say what you need to to get what you want."

"I want you. I want you," he repeated as if she hadn't heard him the first two times. "I've never wanted anything or anyone more. Tell me you don't want me, too."

"I don't—"

"*Liar.* You want me just as much as I want you."

His hands slid to her neck and he pulled her mouth closer to his, but instead of kissing her—something she shamelessly craved—he spoke in a gentle tone against her lips.

"You want me. You want me to kiss you until you're breathless."

"*I don't.*" Though the longing in her tone suggested otherwise.

Dear Reader,

Thank you so much for purchasing my debut Harlequin Kimani Romance title, *In the Market for Love*. I'm superexcited for you to meet Alonso Wright and Vivian Moore. These two spark a flame that blazes a path toward happily-ever-after; however, there are a few bumps along the way.

Alonso doesn't want to admit he's met his match in Vivian, but she can turn his world upside down with a simple glance. Like most powerful men, Alonso believes money can buy anything. But Vivian will show him love is free.

Like the tagline says: every passion has its price.

I hope you enjoy Alonso and Vivian's love story and that their journey toward happiness tickles your heart, touches your emotions and warms your soul.

Thank you for supporting me!

Love and light,

Joy

PS: I love hearing from readers. Email me at authorjoyavery@gmail.com.

In the Market for Love

JOY AVERY

HARLEQUIN® KIMANI™ ROMANCE

Recycling programs
for this product may
not exist in your area.

ISBN-13: 978-0-373-86512-3

In the Market for Love

For questions and comments about the quality of this book please contact us
at CustomerService@Harlequin.com.

HARLEQUIN®
www.Harlequin.com

Printed in U.S.A.

By day, **Joy Avery** works as a customer-service assistant. By night, the North Carolina native travels to imaginary worlds, creating characters whose romantic journeys invariably end happily-ever-after.

Since she was a young girl growing up in Garner, Joy knew she wanted to write. Stumbling onto romance novels, she discovered her passion for love stories and instantly knew those were the type of stories she wanted to pen.

Joy is married with one child. When not writing, she enjoys reading, cake decorating, pretending to expertly play the piano, driving her husband insane and playing with her two dogs.

Books by Joy Avery

Harlequin Kimani Romance

In the Market for Love

Dedicated to the dream.

Acknowledgments

To Marcus:
Thank you for your unwavering support
and your patience and understanding
when I switch into writerzilla mode.

To Avion:
Thank you for the random sticky notes of
encouragement placed around my writing room.

To Paula, aka Lyla Dune:
Thank you for being an awesome critique partner.

To my readers, my tribe, my street team:
What can I say? You guys totally rock and totally roll.
Your support is amazing! I appreciate each and
every one of you. From the bottom of my heart,
THANK YOU! Thank you for your support!
Thank you for your wonderful emails and messages.
Thank you for your encouragement. Thank you for
believing in my love stories and sharing your love
for Joy Avery romances with the world.

To my friends and family:
Thank you for your support!

Chapter 1

Vivian Moore stood at the nurses' station inside Raleigh's Tender Hearts Memorial Hospital, where she'd worked for the past six years, pecking away at the tablet she'd been issued. The newly implemented "convenience" hadn't turned out to be the *inconvenience* she'd originally assumed it would be, after all. *A point for the home team.*

Tuning out the beeping, chiming and chatter swirling around her, she focused on entering the vitals for her last patient of the day. *The last patient of the day.* The thought made her smile. Unfortunately, instead of going home, climbing into bed and sleeping for three days straight, she had to meet with a persistent real estate developer who couldn't seem to take no for an answer over the phone. *Hopefully, face-to-face will do the trick.*

"Vi?"

Only one person ever addressed her by the shortened name—her best friend and fellow ER nurse, Tressa. Vivian turned to see Tressa hurrying toward her, jet-black locks bouncing with each step the petite woman took.

By the expression on Tressa's soft brown face, she'd experienced the unexplainable. Vivian grew concerned. The last time Tressa donned such a look, she'd been socked in the jaw by a disgruntled patient. Well, she wasn't crying. That was a good sign, right?

Vivian pushed her tablet aside. "What's wrong?"

For a second or two, Tressa stood speechless but finally snapped out of her stupor. "I just saw him. And he is fine. I mean, capital-*F* fine." Her eyes did a dreamy flutter. "And chocolate. Deliciously chocolate. *Mmm*."

By *him*, Vivian had no doubt she referred to the drop-dead gorgeous man rumored to be roaming the halls earlier. *Uninterested* had been Vivian's feeling, but if the man's looks had the ability to render Tressa speechless—a task not easily accomplished—then maybe he just might be worthy of all the whispers that had burned through the halls like a wildfire.

Though initially apathetic, she had to admit she was a little curious, until an image of her trifling ex flashed in her head. Her jaw tightened at the mere thought of the man—dog—no-good bastard. If he'd taught her anything, it'd been to never trust a handsome face.

Adopting her previous state of disinterest, Vivian returned her attention to the tablet. But Tressa had other plans for her attention, hooking her arm around Vivian's and venturing down the brightly lit corridor. "Where are we going?"

"You'll see."

"I have work to do, Tress."

"Trust me, this will be well worth the brief distraction."

"I don't—" Vivian stopped abruptly with Tressa directing her attention to the statue of a man several feet away, a cell phone pinned to his ear.

Vivian's eyes raked over his well-put-together body. Six-three, two twenty-five. A calculated guess, but she would wager she was spot-on. His skin was as smooth and dark as the tempered chocolate used on a sinful-desserts show she'd watched earlier that week. Both stirred her hunger, but for totally different reasons.

"You were saying?"

If Vivian had to guess, Tressa was standing with her arms folded across her chest and a smirk on her face. Unfortunately gravity, the universe, lust—she didn't know which—wouldn't allow her to pull her eyes away from *him* to verify.

The way the navy blue suit pants fit his toned lower half, there could be no disputing they'd been custom tailored just for him. Allowing her eyes to roam a bit higher, she fixed on the mound that bulged at his biceps when he bent his arm to massage his neatly groomed beard with two long fingers.

Even with an obstructed view of what lay beneath the crisp blue-and-white pin-striped shirt, she had a good idea it could make her knees knock. Her gaze trailed over his wide shoulders. Never again would she look at suspenders as an old man's accessory.

If by some foolish chance she'd forgotten it'd been close to a year since she'd had sex, the way her body was currently responding would have instantly reminded her. A searing heat—having nothing to do with the June temperature—blossomed in her cheeks, flowed down her body and settled right between her legs.

"Oh, my God, did you just moan?"

Tressa's words snapped Vivian out of her trancelike stare. Vivian shifted toward Tressa. "No—" She cleared her throat. "No, I didn't moan." Had she? With her arms across her chest—just as Vivian had guessed—Tressa flashed her a do-I-look-dumb-to-you expression.

Vivian sighed and rolled her eyes away, inadvertently—

or intentionally, at this point, she didn't know—landing
back on *him* again. *God, you are one good-looking man. I
bet you are all types of trouble.* Had Tressa really labeled
him a *brief* distraction? There was nothing brief about this
man. His entire presence screamed prolonged.

"Ahem."

The sound coming from behind them made every mus-
cle in Vivian's body seize. Only one person in the entire
hospital had that effect on her. Ms. Kasetta. *Busted.* They
both turned slowly to face Tender Hearts's most stern ER
charge nurse.

"Good morning, Ms. Kasetta," said Vivian.

Tressa echoed the greeting.

Ms. Kasetta stood with her hands clasped behind her
back, donning her usual tight scowl. Vivian couldn't recall ever seeing the woman smile. Many joked she'd been
there since Tender Hearts was founded sixty years ago.
The woman may have been hard-nosed, but no one garnered more respect or kept the ER running as flawlessly
as she did.

Ms. Kasetta gave a staunch nod. "Ms. Moore. Ms.
Washington."

When Ms. Kasetta's eyes roamed past them, Vivian
didn't need to follow her stare to know where her gaze had
settled, because something in her firm expression softened.
Obviously she'd experienced the heat wave, too. Vivian bit
back the smile that twitched at the corners of her mouth.

A beat later, Ms. Kasetta's attention returned to them.
"Ms. Moore, where's your name badge?"

Shit. Vivian touched the bare spot her badge usually occupied. "I…must have left it in my locker. I'll get it now."

"See that you do."

Ms. Kasetta sent one more glance in Tempered Chocolate's direction, then was off.

Tressa exhaled as if she'd been holding her breath the entire time. "That woman scares the hell out of me."

Vivian eyed the direction Ms. Kasetta had traveled. "She scares the hell out of everyone."

Tressa performed an animated shiver. "I have to get back to work before Dragon Lady sets me ablaze. You can thank me later."

Vivian shook her head as her friend ambled away. *Thank her? More like strangle her for ever introducing me to this mayhem.* Unable to resist, she dared one last look at Tempered Chocolate.

If the way he paced back and forth and ran his hand over his head was any indication, the call was not going so well. Who was he here to see? Probably a girlfriend or wife. Didn't really matter. To her, he was just something good to look at.

And as if he sensed Vivian's eyes locked to him, he glanced in her direction. She gasped from the unexpected connection. The phone lowered from his ear, but then eased back. All she could do was continue to dumbly ogle him.

Their eyes held for what she'd label an eternity. Had her feet not been rooted to the industrial tile, she would have darted away. Luckily, the blaring ding that always preceded an overhead announcement sounded, jolting her from the paralyzed state. Hurrying away, she escaped to the locker room to retrieve her badge and decompress.

Inside the dimly lit room, Vivian searched everywhere: her gym bag, her purse, the floor. No badge. She was certain she'd packed it. Well, almost certain. Finally settling on the fact the badge was MIA she tossed her head back and released an audible sigh.

The thought of the judgmental look Ms. Kasetta would undoubtedly toss her once she confessed she'd lost yet another badge made Vivian sigh even more heavily. Maybe she could make it to human resources and have one printed before she ran into the daunting woman again.

Vivian dug into her wallet for a twenty. It was no secret the implementation of the fee for replacement badges was a result of her inability to keep up with the dreaded thing.

The locker room door swung open, and Vivian jolted. Her coworker Gemma rushed inside.

"Oh, thank goodness. I found you."

Vivian was afraid to ask why the woman sought her. Whatever the reason, it undoubtedly meant more work for Vivian. "What can I do for you?" The question of doom.

"Can you take my patient in bay fourteen? Please, please, please. He's homeless, and you're good with them. And he smells. The stench never seems to bother you." Her voice lowered to a whisper. "You know I'm pregnant. I can't take the odor. I'd throw up everywhere. It wouldn't be professional to throw up on a patient. I'll owe you lots and lots. Anything. Any—"

Vivian flashed her palm to pause an anxious Gemma. Four years in North Carolina and the woman still had the deepest New Orleans accent. It seemed to grow deeper whenever she got excited—like now.

"Calm down, momma. I'll do it." *So much for last patient of the day.* Vivian rested her hand on Gemma's not-yet-protruding stomach. "All this excitement is no good for the baby."

"I know. I just get so overwhelmed sometimes. You're a lifesaver, Vivian. I don't know what I'd do without you."

Tears clouded Gemma's eyes. Pregnancy had turned the usually take-no-prisoners woman into a bundle of emotions. Vivian truly didn't mind. With her work at the homeless shelter and time spent volunteering at the soup kitchen, plus working in a hospital setting, she'd become nose blind to most odors.

Rubbing Gemma's shoulders, she said, "You know I've

got your back, girl. Stay here and get yourself together. I'll be in to check on you once I'm done. Okay?"

A crimson-faced Gemma nodded and rubbed at her eyes.

Outside the locker room, Vivian sighed. She honestly felt sympathy for the woman. Once her boyfriend had learned she was pregnant, he'd taken off and left her. *What in the hell is wrong with men these days?*

Unlike most hospitals, Tender Hearts's "bays" were actual rooms and not the customary dismal curtains that separated individuals in the ER. The second Vivian entered Mr. Hamilton Price's room the odor of sweat and hard living hit her.

Yes, it was enough to water your eyes, but nothing she couldn't handle. Compared to the things she'd smelled in the past, this was pine cleaner. The instant her eyes landed on the scruffy man reclined in the bed, she recognized him from the soup kitchen where she volunteered.

Mr. Price's salt-and-pepper hair hung in locks down his back. She wasn't sure if his dark, leathery skin was a result of the elements or time. If nothing else, he certainly appeared to eat well, and that made her happy. The thought of anyone going hungry troubled her.

"Mr. Price?"

He rotated his head toward her. A smile lifted the corners of his mouth, revealing several missing teeth on the bottom and a bit of decay on the others.

"That's me, pretty lady. Come on over here closer so I can see you a little better."

Vivian smiled and neared the bed. "Well, you know, Mr. Price—"

"Call me Hamilton. Mr. Price was my father. Boy, he was an ornery SOB."

He laughed—*ta-hee-hee*—or at least Vivian thought it was laughter.

"Yep, an ornery SOB, but a good man. Not many of them around these days, good men."

He didn't have to try to convince her. She totally agreed. Calling the mature gentleman by his first name felt disrespectful, but she did as instructed and honored his wishes. "*Hamilton*, if you took your diabetes medication like you're supposed to, you wouldn't have this blurry vision. You'd be able to see me clear across the room."

He laughed again. "Oh, I like you already. Feisty. And I know someone else who'd like you, too. You know them good men I—"

Before Hamilton completed his thought, the door crept open behind them. When Vivian rotated, time came to a standstill. *Him. Tempered Chocolate.* The second their gazes collided, her body performed a similar shameful act as before. But added to the searing heat that rushed through her system, again, her nipples tightened inside her bra.

No, no, no, don't you dare betray me like this, she warned her defiant body.

Questions flooded her. Had he entered the wrong room? Was he lost? Or less likely, had he been looking for her? She mentally drop-kicked the latter thought from her head. *How ridiculous. Of course he isn't looking for me.*

Sadly, their connection now didn't reflect the one they'd shared earlier—at least judging by his expression. In fact, now he seemed downright bothered by her presence. Vivian thought she even detected a hint of a scowl on his gorgeous face. But why? The only interaction they'd had before this moment had been a glance—a look—okay, a heat-packed, center-stirring stare, which at the time he'd seemed to appreciate just as much as she had. Obviously something had changed.

"*Ta-hee-hee*. Just as I expected," came from Hamilton's direction.

Vivian wasn't sure what Hamilton's comment meant,

but it was enough to draw Tempered's demanding eyes away from her. A good thing, too. Another second and she would have needed an IV. This man's presence was draining. And to make it worse, though they hadn't spoken a single word to one another, he had her body in a tailspin.

Chocolate had always been her weakness.

Chapter 2

Alonso Wright stopped dead in his tracks the second he entered Hamilton's room. *Her.* The beautiful nurse he'd caught staring at him earlier. Okay, he couldn't confirm for sure she'd been staring, but she'd certainly appeared guilty when his eyes had met hers. He was pretty sure she'd gasped, too.

Normally he would have appreciated the fact he'd been given another opportunity to admire the way her brown hair dangled in the ponytail every time she moved her head, or how her pecan-toned skin shimmered under the fluorescent lighting, or the hungry way her innocent-looking brown eyes drank him up. Unfortunately, the way the rude nurse who'd been here earlier had darted from the room overshadowed it all.

From the moment the other nurse had entered the room, she'd acted as if Hamilton's mere existence disgusted her. Recalling the way the woman had rushed from the room, while Alonso was in midsentence, angered him all over again. She'd disrespected him, but more important, had disrespected Hamilton.

Was this her replacement? This one was probably just as unsympathetic as the one before. He'd hate to have to make a phone call about her, too. In a dry tone, he said, "I buzzed for someone over fifteen minutes ago. I'm glad you finally decided to grace us with your presence."

"I apologize, sir. But I'm here now."

"Well, we don't need you now. I handled your job for you." He lifted the can of soda he'd been holding, then neared Hamilton's bedside.

She moved beside him with the speed of a cheetah. "Uh, what are you doing?"

"I'm making sure my friend doesn't dehydrate, since I'm the only one who seems concerned about his well-being." He normally wasn't this sour, but a mixture of worry, stress and thin patience with the staff had him not his usual self. Maybe he needed a Snickers.

The bold woman confiscated the can of soda before he could pass it to Hamilton. "Hamilton can't have this. We're trying to *lower* his blood sugar, not increase it. Which is exactly what this would do."

Hamilton? Were they on a first-name basis? "Well, if I could have gotten one of you to actually respond, maybe we would have had a more viable option. And it's *Mr. Price*. He deserves the same respect you'd give any other patient in this hospital." Alonso shook his head. "You people are something else. And for the record, he has good health insurance. Great insurance, actually. Probably better than yours. So you can stop treating him like a second-class citizen and do your job."

When her jaw muscles flexed and her brown eyes turned a shade darker, Alonso knew he'd hit a nerve. But he wasn't backing down.

"*Ta-hee-hee.* Uh-oh. I think you done poked the hornet's nest, boy."

Yep, it appeared so. After a couple seconds more of boring a hole in him with those mesmerizing eyes, she slid her attention from Alonso to Hamilton. A warm smile curled her lips as she addressed him.

"Hamilton…"

Alonso didn't miss the fact that she'd cut her eyes at him with the use of Hamilton's first name again.

"Sodas aren't a good option. They may be okay every once in a while, but they're loaded with sugar. Which I'm sure you know wreaks havoc on your diabetes."

"Yeah. I tried to tell that knucklehead."

Alonso's brows furrowed. *What?* Hamilton had thrown him under the bus. He'd been the one to ask for the damn soda. At the smirk on Hamilton's face, Alonso shook his head. When the nurse tossed a disapproving glance in Alonso's direction, Alonso folded his arms across his chest and remained silent. That seemed like the best option.

Rolling her eyes away, she wrapped a blood pressure cuff around Hamilton's thin arm.

"Don't worry. Once I check your vitals, I'll get you something more suitable."

Hamilton smiled so wide Alonso thought the corners of his mouth would split.

"Thank you, darling. Smart, pretty and accommodating. You married? Now, you're a little too young for me. What are you, twenty-five, twenty-six?"

"Thirty-four, actually."

Alonso was just as stunned as Hamilton appeared. The woman didn't look anywhere close to thirty. Obviously good genes. At the mention of genes, Alonso's eyes lowered to her ass. Yeah, definitely good genes. And he wouldn't mind being the pair of jeans that got to cup all of that. Something stirred in the pit of his stomach, but he chose to ignore it.

"You'd be perfect for—" Hamilton cut his eye to Alonso "—someone else I know."

Alonso flashed him a scowl. The man never missed an opportunity to play matchmaker. Even if Alonso were interested in her—which he wasn't—he didn't see her being a no-commitment type of woman. Thanks to his ex, commitment no longer interested him.

She chuckled. "Say 'ahh,' Hamilton."

Neither Hamilton's scent nor tattered clothing seemed to bother her. Her gentle manner with Hamilton forced Alonso to consider the fact he may have pegged her all wrong. Her compassion toward Hamilton appeared actually genuine. Or maybe it was because Alonso had called her out earlier. Either way, he was glad Hamilton was getting the respect he deserved.

Alonso recalled the way he'd treated her earlier. *Damn.* He regretted the fact he'd been such an asshole. Maybe he'd get the chance to make it right.

"All right. We're all done here. Quick and painless. Now for that drink. Water, unsweetened tea, coffee, diet soda?"

Alonso rocked back on his heels. "So many delicious choices." It was his chance to smirk when Hamilton eyed him. *Payback for the earlier jab.* If the nurse wasn't in the room, Alonso was sure Hamilton would have flipped him the bird. That was their relationship. They gave each other shit, but Alonso trusted the man with his life. Hell, he had Hamilton to thank for his life.

"Can I get you anything?"

Her voice tore into Alonso's thoughts, snatching him from the past. "I'm sorry?"

"Would you like something to drink?"

The offer surprised Alonso, until he considered she probably planned to poison him. Despite their earlier confrontation—if you could call it that—her manner toward him wasn't hostile. Quite the opposite, in fact. He noted kindness in her expression. Yeah, she planned to poison him. "Ahh…no. I'm good. Thank you, though."

"Sit tight, Hamilton. I'll be right back."

With that, she turned and headed toward the door. Alonso couldn't help but observe the sway of her shapely hips. It'd been too long since he'd held on to curves like hers.

"Put your tongue in. *Ta-hee-hee.* You handled that like a pro. Don't know how to handle a woman who doesn't fall at your feet, huh?"

Alonso chuckled. "Look here, old man, you just focus on getting better and not my effect on women."

"Old man? Don't make me get out of this bed and show you an old man. Old man, my ass."

Alonso laughed. The only thing Hamilton hated more than being told what to do was being called old. After a few moments of laughter, Alonso sobered. Pulling the cushioned chair bedside, he eased into it. "We need to talk, Ham," he said, using the nickname he'd called Hamilton for years.

"*Uh-oh.* I know where this is going."

Alonso was sure he sounded like a broken record. He'd had the same conversation with Hamilton numerous times. But now, things were different. "The streets are no good for you."

"I can take care of myself. Been doing it for years. Even saved your ass a time or two."

Truth. Alonso's thoughts drifted seventeen years into the past, to the night he was sure Hamilton referred to. The night Hamilton had saved him from being stabbed to death. The night that had anchored the two men for life, as far as Alonso was concerned. The night—even after all these years—that still occasionally woke him in a cold sweat.

Like a phantom, Hamilton had appeared in the dark alley just in time. After subduing two of the three thugs, he'd rushed the third. Unfortunately, not before the guy had stabbed Alonso. Alonso unconsciously smoothed a hand down his side. He still wore the jagged scar of that horrific night. Yeah, he owed Hamilton his life.

Alonso brushed a hand over his head. "Things have changed, Ham. You're—"

"Things like what?"

"Your health for one." Alonso chastised himself for the raised tone. Hamilton turned onto his side, and Alonso was forced to stare at his back. "Ham, when I got the call you'd been found unconscious and rushed to the hospital—" A sinking feeling rushed over Alonso, forcing him to pause. Gathering himself, he continued, "I thought you were dead. It scared the hell out of me." It was the call he'd dreaded receiving ever since he'd given Hamilton a cell phone and stored his number as the emergency contact. Alonso dropped his head. In a muted tone, he repeated, "It scared the hell out of me."

Hamilton faced him again, a smile curling his chapped lips. "I love you, too, young buck. Don't worry 'bout me. It'll take more than high blood sugar to take me out."

It was always the *more* Alonso worried about. Alonso rested his elbow on his thighs and eyed the man. Hamilton was his late grandfather reincarnated—stubborn, overly independent and reluctant to accept help from anyone… including him. Yep, Hamilton reminded him so much of the man who'd raised him. Perhaps that was why he felt so attached to him. So damn tenacious.

"You better not let that one slip away," Hamilton said.

Alonso shot him a don't-start-with-me expression.

"Don't look at me like that. I sensed the attraction between the two of you. Thought I was gon' catch fire from those licking flames."

Attraction was a stretch. Alonso shot a quick glance at the door. Shouldn't she be back by now? He set his sights on Ham again. "Quit trying to change the subject."

"Quit sounding like a broken record."

Alonso's phone chimed, indicating an incoming message. He fished it from his pocket but turned his attention back to Hamilton before checking it. "It's time, Ham. An apartment, a condo, a house, I'll get you whatever you want. I just need you off the streets. Don't make me beg."

Hamilton eyed him long and hard. "Well, if it'll get you to stop hounding me…I'll consider it."

Alonso clapped Hamilton's shoulder, then checked the reminder message from his assistant. *Shit.* He'd forgotten all about his appointment with Vivian Moore. Trying to get that damn woman's house was going to prematurely gray him. At thirty-seven, he was too young to be a silver fox.

The one-o'clock appointment should still be doable. *If the doctor ever decides to make an appearance.* He checked his watch. At eleven in the morning, he was cutting it close. Maybe he should reschedule while there was still plenty of time to do so. Keying a message to his assistant to contact Ms. Moore with his regrets and to reschedule, he stuffed the device back into his pocket.

And speaking of appearances… He shot another glance at the door. Where in the hell did she have to go for the bottle of water?

As if his words had summoned her, she strolled in. Their eyes met again in that heated way that seemed to have become customary with them. His heartbeat quickened. What the hell was that? He cleared his throat, then broke their connection.

She placed Hamilton's water on the small table next to the bed. Resting her thin hand on his forearm, she said, "All right, Hamilton. If you need anything, just buzz the desk." Her eyes found Alonso's. "And I'll instruct them to page me immediately." Focus back on Hamilton, she continued, "The doctor should be in shortly. Hopefully after his visit you'll be outta here to enjoy this beautiful weather."

"Thank you, sweetheart. You're a jewel. No one with good sense would let you slip away."

Alonso breathed a sigh of relief when Hamilton didn't look in his direction. The man had embarrassed him enough for one day. Before the nurse made it out of the room, Alonso was out of his chair. He owed her an apology.

"Excuse me." She stopped, but didn't turn to face him. "I'm sorry I didn't catch your name—"

She swiveled to face him. "Busy."

The temperature in the room dropped about twenty degrees. Obviously she still held a slight grudge.

Her gaze drifted past him momentarily to Hamilton. "He's going to be okay."

A blink later, she was gone. But only from the room, because the spirited nurse still lingered in Alonso's thoughts.

Chapter 3

Vivian cracked her window to get some fresh air. It was all she could do to keep her eyes open. The ER had been busier than she'd experienced in months. Definitely not typical for a Tuesday.

A shift that should have ended at seven in the morning hadn't ended until ten. Then she'd had to rush home, change clothes and dart across town. If she'd had any sense at all, she would have canceled the appointment with Mr. Wright.

It wasn't like he hadn't canceled on her a week ago, citing a family emergency. *Yeah, right.* He'd probably flown off to some exotic island with his mistress. Obviously money wasn't a problem since he seemed to like sending people unsolicited checks.

Men.

At the mention of men, her thoughts floated to one man in particular. The one she'd thought about for the past week. Hamilton's...*guardian*, she guessed would be an appropriate term. She no longer thought of him as Tempered Chocolate. Tempered Chocolate suited a more delectable individual. His inexcusable attack on her was anything but appetizing.

"Did he really think he could tell me how to do a job I've performed for twelve years?"

The nerve of him.

A wave of frustration rippled through her. Oh, she'd wanted so badly to tear into him. Thankfully, her grandmother had taught her not to waste her words on people who didn't deserve her attention. Then there was the small issue of needing her job.

She had to admit, overhearing—kinda eavesdropping on—the conversation he'd been having with Hamilton about getting off the street redeemed him a little. While he'd been an ass to her, he'd seemed to genuinely care about Hamilton.

How'd the two know each other? Judging by the tailored suit and expensive shoes, he didn't strike her as someone who favored the homeless. *Ugh. There you go judging people again.* Her grandmother would have been disappointed.

A reel of her Nina—the name she'd dubbed her spirited grandmother—played in her head. "God, I miss you."

She parked a little more than a block from her favorite Mexican restaurant, where she'd agreed to meet Alonso Wright. *In and out*, she reminded herself as she reached for the door handle of her Toyota Avalon, but not before double-checking to make sure she hadn't forgotten the envelope containing the check from Wright Developing. Apparently, Mr. Wright assumed all the zeros would tempt her. Well, he was about to find out his money couldn't buy everything.

As she strolled down Blount Street, Vivian was glad she'd worn the flat sandals. *A good call.* The one thing downtown Raleigh could really use more of was parking.

She didn't mind the trek, though. The temperature was a comfortable eighty-three degrees.

There were a hundred other things she could have been doing—namely sleeping—instead of wasting her time telling Mr. Wright the same thing she'd told him five times previously.

In and out.

Checking her watch, she saw she was twenty minutes early for the 11:45 meeting. The second she ambled into the restaurant, the delicious aroma of sizzling fajitas invaded her nostrils. Her stomach growled, reminding her she'd skipped breakfast…again.

By the number of meals she'd missed working in the ER, she should be no more than a hundred pounds. Not the hundred and forty-three she proudly flaunted.

"*Hola*, Vivian."

At the sound of her name, Vivian turned to see Hector, the proprietor of Caliente Mexicana, approaching her. Hector was a little shy of five feet and round as a whiskey barrel. But what he lacked in appearance, he made up for in personality. Over the four years she'd been a patron there, she'd gotten to know the sixty-year-old well. "*Hola*, Hector. *Cómo estás?*"

"*Muy bien. Y tu?*"

"*Muy agotado.*" A look of distress spread across Hector's face, and Vivian knew it was genuine concern.

"Why very exhausted?" he asked in accented English.

"Work."

"I understand. I'll put you in *un rincón muy tranquilo*," he said, gesturing with his hands.

Any other day she would have welcomed a very quiet booth in the corner. "That's thoughtful, Hector, but I'm meeting someone."

"Ah. The *hermoso* gentleman."

She wasn't sure whether or not Mr. Wright was handsome, but Hector obviously thought so. "Gentleman, I hope. Handsome, I don't know." She lowered her voice. "I've never met him."

"Ah. You will be pleased. I'll take you to him."

"Wait. He's here already?"

"Sí."

Guess she wasn't the only one who liked being punctual.

Vivian smoothed a hand down the front of the sleeveless green-and-white maxi dress she wore, a sudden bout of nerves fluttering in her stomach. She inhaled a deep breath, then released it slowly. Why was she so uneasy? It wasn't like this was a first date. Any kind of date, for that matter.

When her eyes landed on the man sitting alone at the secluded table, she froze. *No freaking way.* She didn't believe in coincidences. Fate, yes. But not coincidences. And right now, her belief in fate was up for examination.

This had to be a mistake. There was no way on God's green earth the jerk from the hospital and the Alonso Wright she was there to meet were one and the same.

Impossible.

After a quick scan of the area to see if maybe Hector had confused the two men, she had her answer. Her horoscope had said today she'd face new challenges. She certainly hadn't prepared for this degree of complication.

This didn't change anything. If anything, it made what she needed to do easier. The man had already rubbed her the wrong way once; she wouldn't give him another opportunity.

Mr. Wright glanced up from his device and did what she labeled a triple take. Yep, he was baffled, too. God, he made mystified look so good.

Their eyes locked from across the room. To say she experienced a jolt of attraction would be putting it mildly.

The man was gorgeous. Really gorgeous. Runway-model gorgeous. Too bad he was such an asshole.

She wanted to snatch her eyes away, but his dark gaze held her like a powerful magnet. When he stood, her breath caught in her throat. The suit clung to his body like fine art. Yes, she was captivated. And underdressed for the occasion, apparently. Her eyes weren't the only set appreciating the human form. Her cheeks warmed under his scrutiny.

"Are you okay?"

Vivian shifted toward Hector, thankful he'd broken the spell. *"Sí."* It was all she could do to force her feet to take her forward and not back. Luckily, they cooperated, placing her toe-to-toe with *him*, Tempered Chocolate, jerk from the hospital, Alonso Wright.

With a narrow-eyed gaze, he said, "Have…we met before?"

Apparently, his curiosity trumped a customary greeting. Had they met before? Really? So much for making a lasting first impression. In her defense, at the hospital she'd worn scrubs, her hair in a ponytail and no makeup.

"Actually, yes, we have. You rudely alluded to me being the worst nurse you'd ever encountered."

"The hospital," he said more to himself than to Vivian. A look of regret spread across his face. "Mrs. Wright—" He lowered his head and chuckled.

Had he just given her his last name? *Vivian Wright. Not bad.* Urgently, she reminded herself why she was there. Business, not lust.

His head slowly rose. "I'm sorry about that. It's been a long day. Mrs. *Moore* is what I actually meant to say."

"No worries. And it's *Ms.* Wright—" Vivian's eyes widened. *Shit.* "Moore. It's Ms. Moore." Why was she cracking under pressure? She was an ER nurse. Pressure was her middle name. When Alonso flashed one of the sexiest smiles she'd ever seen, she temporarily changed her name to woman-who-couldn't-control-her-libido.

Alonso shrugged. "See, accidents happen."

"Amor a primera vista," Hector said, before leaving them alone.

Love at first sight? Not hardly.

"We started off on the wrong foot. I'd really like the opportunity to redeem myself and apologize for my behavior at the hospital." He extended his arm toward her. "Alonso Wright."

When Vivian's palm rested against his, a searing heat rushed up her arm. Ignoring the tingle, she forced out, "Vivian Moore."

Alonso eyed her as if attempting to memorize her features. A beat later, he jerked as if he'd realized he'd been staring at her, then released her hand.

"Ah…sit, please."

Her brain almost processed the command. Luckily, good sense kicked in. "I won't be staying. I wanted to return this." She rummaged through her oversize purse, fished out the envelope and passed it to him. "My answer last month was no. My answer last week was no. My answer today is still no. Enjoy the rest of your day, Mr. Wright." She turned and started away.

"Three hundred thousand."

Vivian stopped. Three hundred thousand was double what he'd originally offered. She faced him, then slowly moved back to the table. "I'm sure there are plenty of other properties in North Carolina that would suit you. Why do you want mine so badly?" Word on the street was he'd already acquired every house in her old neighborhood except hers.

A glint of vulnerability sparked in his eyes, and she couldn't help but wonder why. Especially since everything about this man screamed resilient—from his confident dark eyes and square jaw, to his enticing lips and strong chin.

"I'm offering more than you would ever get for the property, Ms. Moore."

Vivian noted how he'd skirted around her question. "I'm sorry, Mr. Wright. It's not for sale. And neither am I."

He frowned. "Is that what you think I'm doing? Trying to buy you."

She fanned her hand around the colorful restaurant. "Isn't that what this lunch is all about? Wine and dine me to get what you want."

Alonso released a sexy chuckle that caressed her body like gentle fingers.

"Wine and dine you, huh?" He massaged his chin with two fingers and smiled. "Something tells me you're worth far more than a chimichanga."

"And that something would be absolutely correct. Good day, Mr. Wright."

There was no way Alonso was letting Ms. Moore slip away. Not just because he needed to convince her to sell, but because something about the woman drew him in and dangled him like prey over the mouth of a hungry, lust-filled beast.

He never mixed business with pleasure, but he'd be lying if he said he didn't like the idea of spending a few pleasure-filled nights with her. Despite the potent desire to take her right there on the table, he refused to allow his craving to cloud his judgment. A lot rode on this deal.

With the money he'd already invested into the project— downtown shops, restaurants, a hotel and the most important landmark, a swanky event center to honor his grandfather— he stood to lose a lot of money. He didn't like to lose at anything.

Think, Wright. Get her to stay.

"You owe me a soda." When he folded his arms across his chest, her eyes drifted to his biceps, then shot up to meet his. So, he wasn't the only one gripped by temptation.

"Excuse me?"

"You owe me a soda. At the hospital, you confiscated my soda and never returned it. I worked hard for that soda. You owe me a replacement." Of course, he wasn't serious, but the quizzical way she eyed him suggested she thought he was. He'd pay triple what he was already offering just to know what was racing through her head.

"Okay, then." She dug into her purse. "How much do I owe you? A dollar? A dollar fifty? How about I give you two?"

Well, that hadn't gone the way he'd intended. He'd expected a laugh, a smile, some show of amusement. Alonso touched her arm and his skin prickled. *What the...?* Suddenly, the temperature in the restaurant rose about ten degrees. If he started to sweat, he would sizzle and steam. How embarrassing would that be? He couldn't remember the last time—or if ever—his body had reacted this way.

"Ms. *Wr*— Moore." *Shit.* Why did he keep giving her his last name? "I was only kidding. I don't want your money. We have a lunch appointment." He shrugged. "Why not have lunch?"

Vivian mimicked his stance. "Instead of lunch, perhaps you should go home and get some rest. You keep confusing me with your sister. I'm certainly not old enough to be confused for your mother."

Ah. She did have a sense of humor. "I'm an only child, and my mother is deceased."

Panic spread across her face. "Oh. I'm sorry. I didn't—"

"You can make it up to me." He pulled out her chair. "And as an incentive, I'll tell you how I thought you were an eighty-year-old woman." The revelation seemed to pique her curiosity.

"An eighty-year-old woman?" She eased into the chair. "This should be good."

Score.

After placing their orders, they feasted on chips and salsa while Alonso told her how he'd chatted with the elderly woman from her old neighborhood—before he'd purchased her house. She'd told him stories about a Vivian Moore who'd lived across the street.

"You must have talked to Ms. Marla. She's a bit senile. I think she had me confused with my great-grandmother. I'm named after her." Her brow arched. "Did I sound eighty over the phone?"

"You never really said a whole lot. An *mmm-hmm* here and an *uh-huh* there. Now that I think about it, you kinda reminded me of an old lady."

Vivian tossed a crumpled napkin at him, then laughed. If he had to guess, she was warming up to him. "See, I'm not so bad after all, right?"

The look she flashed him suggested she wasn't wholly convinced of the claim. Well, Rome wasn't built in a day.

Their food arrived. The chips and salsa were good, but hadn't been enough. The cheesy beef-tip burrito would do the trick. He tried to ignore how tempting it was to watch Vivian take a forkful of the grilled-chicken taco salad into her mouth. Yeah, he envied the utensil.

Breaking the silence, he said, "I get it, Ms. Moore. You have a sentimental attachment to your childhood home. It's understandable. But you don't need me to tell you that three hundred thousand is a *very* generous offer."

She eyed him a moment. Was she mulling it over?

"What do you intend to construct on the site, Mr. Wright?"

"Excuse me?"

"I asked what you intend on constructing on the site. You've purchased all of the homes, with the exception of mine, of course. I doubt you plan on renovating. So… what's your plan?"

Her eyes narrowed on him as if she were attempting to read his mind. And for a moment, he experienced a hint of unease. Was he allowing this no-more-than one-hundred-forty-pound nurse to rattle him?

"Let me guess. Condos? Fancy restaurants? Stores no one in that community could even afford to shop in?"

"Jobs."

By the slight softening of her features, it was the last answer she'd expected. He placed his fork down and dabbed at the corners of his mouth. "You have me all wrong, Vivian. May I call you Vivian?"

She nodded.

"There are many things you don't see when you look at me. Just as I'm sure there are many layers to you." And he'd like to peel them all away.

"Maybe. What forms will these jobs—"

In a bold move, he reached across and brushed a crumb from her cheek. When his finger grazed her warm skin, she stilled. Yeah, they had something going on, sparks. By her bewildered expression, she realized it, too.

She jerked away from his reach, then placed her napkin on the table. "Well—" She cleared her throat. "Well, Alonso. May I call you Alonso?"

He nodded.

"Thank you for lunch. I should really be going." She scooted her chair away from the table, stood, and started to walk away.

Alonso stood. "Would you like your purse?"

Vivian stopped. When she turned, a sheepish expression lingered on her beautiful face. If he didn't know better, he'd rattled her. The notion caused an inward smile. He passed her the black patent-leather bag. "You'll think about my offer?" *And me?* Of course, he didn't say the latter aloud.

"No."

No. "No?"

"Your attempt at softening me, then swooping in for the kill failed." She shrugged. "Sorry. Better luck next time. And by next time, I do mean with someone else, because my answer is final." She smiled and made a hasty escape from the building.

Alonso massaged the side of his face as if he'd been slapped. In a way, he had. Seemed he'd met his match in Vivian Moore. In more ways than one. But he was Alonso Wright. He wouldn't allow this minor roadblock to trouble him. Everyone had a price. He just needed to discover hers.

He smirked. Doing so could be fun.

Chapter 4

Alonso stood at the 3-D table model of his newest development venture: a luxury hotel, condos, eateries and, most important, an event center named after his late grandfather. This was truly the one thing that made the project worthwhile.

He moved away from the table and stood at the floor-to-ceiling window, homing in on one area in particular. "No other location will do," he whispered to himself. To be able to stand in this very spot and glance out to see his grandfather's name featured prominently on the event center... "No, no other spot will do," he repeated to himself. A wave of emotion crashed over him when he thought about how much he missed the man.

Phalonius Wright had been a good man—a great man—and the fact that Alonso was able to honor his grandfather in such a manner swelled him with pride. He'd come a long way and had the man who'd raised him to thank. And this was his way of doing so.

He folded his arms across his chest, his thoughts shifting to Vivian. Why in the hell was the woman being so stubborn? The damn house was falling down. And it wasn't like anyone had occupied the dilapidated dwelling for years. Plus, he was offering her far more than the hovel was worth.

"What's up, bro?"

He turned to see Roth Lexington, his best friend since kindergarten, stroll through his office door. When the tall man stood within arm's reach, Alonso exchanged a manly hug with him. "What's up, man? I thought you were out of town."

"Got back last night." Roth's attention shifted to the layout. "Damn. When you said you were honoring your grandpops, you really meant you were honoring your grandpops. Man…this is amazing." Roth eyed him. "I'm proud of you, dude. And you're making your grandpops real proud, too."

Alonso nodded. "Thanks, man. That means a lot." He eyed his brainchild again. "Out of every project I've done, this is the one that means the most."

"Any luck with the house you need to acquire to seal the deal?"

Alonso sighed heavily. "I'm in trouble, man." He dropped into one of the two coffee-colored leather chairs.

"What do you need?"

This was one of the things Alonso respected most about Roth. He was a helluva friend. It was never *What did you do?* or *What did you get yourself into?* or any bullshit like that. It was always an instant *How can I help?* response.

Alonso leaned forward, resting his elbows on his knees. "I've finally met her."

"Met who?"

"The woman who's going to be my ultimate demise."

"Damn." Roth took a seat adjacent Alonso. "This I've got to hear."

Alonso spent the next hour telling Roth all about Vivian. From his horrible first impression at the hospital, to his scaring her off at the restaurant, and ending with his overwhelming attraction to her.

"Damn. That's wild. The nurse turns out to be the same woman who owns the house."

"I know, right? Sounds like something you'd see on a damn soap opera."

"Sounds like destiny to me. Like it's been determined for you two to connect with each other."

"You sound like Ham. He all but told the woman I wanted her." Alonso ran a hand over his head. "The strange part about it, I can't stop thinking about her. I even dreamed about her last night." He'd awakened harder than a piece of steel.

"Oh, yeah, she's under your skin. You gonna pursue it?"

Alonso shrugged. "Nah. You know I never mix business with pleasure. But there's something about this one I'm having a hard time ignoring. And damn, I've tried."

Roth grinned. "Maybe she's the one."

Alonso laughed. "I don't know about all of that. And I'm damn sure not looking for a relationship. I've traveled that dark road before. But I won't lie, I did enjoy spending time with Vivian." *Despite how brief it may have been.*

"Inez was a long time ago, Lo," Roth said, using the nickname he'd called Alonso since they were tykes. "You can't run from love—or destiny—" he smirked "—forever."

"Says the man who dodges relationships like bullets."

"I'm not dodging. I'm just waiting on the right one. She's out there. But this ain't about me. You gotta stop living in the past. Yeah, it was low-down what Inez did to you, but let it go. You're a good brother, one of the best brothers I know. You deserve a happily-ever-after."

"You sound like a greeting card."

Alonso pushed to his feet and stood in front of the window again. *Inez*. Damn, some women knew how to really break a man. "I trusted that woman. Trusting a woman. My first mistake."

"You didn't make the mistake. She did. You should have been able to trust her. She was your lady." Roth came to stand by Alonso. "You can't condemn every woman because of the actions of one."

Alonso didn't argue because Roth was right. However, Alonso would have never pegged his ex as someone who'd poke holes in his condoms in hopes of securing a wedding proposal—or a payday. He still wasn't truly sure which one she'd been after. She got neither, a wedding nor a baby.

Dammit, he did get to condemn, even if inside he knew he was wrong for doing so. All women weren't the same. He knew that. But remembering what Inez had done to him made that hard to remember.

"I have to stay away from this woman. I fade when I'm near her and become this sensitive, all-in-my-feelings brother. I don't know what she does to me, but I don't like it."

"Sounds to me like she's tapping into the true you. The one you try so desperately to hide from the world."

Roth knew him better than anyone, so there was no use in trying to dispute the claim. He did hide himself. And for good reason. The only side people needed to see of him was his fearless businessman persona. Revealing any other side made him vulnerable. Not even his ex had seen the true depths of him. Why would he allow Vivian to? "I would never give a woman that kind of power over me."

Roth laughed. "Never say never, man."

"In this case, never is a damn good bet. Besides, Vivian Moore seems utterly unimpressed with either face of Alonso Wright."

"Are you sure about that? The way you said she ran from the restaurant when you touched her makes me believe she's not as unimpressed as you think."

Yeah, his touch had seemed to stir something inside her. But was it interest or disgust? "There's no interest there. Trust me. I've called her several times and she hasn't returned even one of my messages."

"Invite her to dinner?"

Had Roth not just heard a word he'd said? "Invite her to dinner?"

"Yes. If you want to gauge her interest, invite her to dinner. If she's not interested, as you suggest, she'll flat out turn you down. If she is interested, she'll pretend not to be but will ultimately say yes." Roth pressed his hand into his chest. "I personally think she's very interested. And to downplay her interest, she'll probably toss out something along the lines of, 'Well, a girl has gotta eat' or 'My mother taught me to never turn down a free meal.'"

Alonso laughed at Roth's animated delivery. "You're a fool, you know that?"

"I've been called worse."

Alonso released a heavy breath. This sounded an awful lot like chasing. Him chasing a woman... Not gonna happen. Hell, women chased him, not the other way around. And even if he bumped his head and decided to take Roth's advice, there was still one small problem: the woman was ignoring him, which for some reason annoyed the shit out of him.

Why was he letting Vivian get to him? Any other woman would have long lost his attention. *Why not her? What is so different about this one?* Questions plagued him. He wouldn't go as far as to say his interest in Vivian scared him, but it damn sure rattled him a bit. The notion made him laugh at himself. *Alonso Wright, rattled by a female.* This shit was a first, and wrong on so many levels.

He needed to reclaim his manhood. "Nah, dinner's not an option. I have to think with the right head on this one. Keep the bigger picture in sight. I need her property. That's the goal. The only one that matters. Strictly business." Though it was truly less about business than it was about his own need. Possibly a selfish one. He didn't have to glance in Roth's direction to know he was flashing a disapproving look. "Go 'head and say it." And as expected, Roth didn't hesitate.

"Forget about business when it comes to happiness."

"Shit. Happiness *is* business, because business equals money. And money makes everybody happy."

Both men turned to see Garth Garrison entering the office. Garth was the builder Alonso typically contracted. They'd started out in the industry roughly around the same time and had tossed each other plenty of business along the way. He stood well over six feet with a commanding presence that always seemed to work in his favor when it came to getting dealings handled.

Garth eyed the 3-D model. "And this piece of business is going to make us a shitload of cold, hard cash."

"Garrison," Alonso said, addressing the man by his last name. He stuck out his hand as the man approached. "You better not have been out there flirting with my assistant again."

Garth laughed. "Can I help it if she wants me?"

"To what do I owe this honor?" Alonso asked.

Before Garth answered, Roth clapped Alonso on the shoulder. "I'm going to head out, man. I just stopped by to say what's up. I'll catch up with you later."

Alonso wasn't sure what the deal was with Roth and Garth, but whenever Garth came around, Roth always made himself scarce. "Okay, man. Are we still on for B-ball this weekend?"

"Absolutely. Gentlemen."

As Roth moved past, Garth chuckled in what Alonso took as a condescending manner. Obviously the man had no idea Roth was one hornet's nest you didn't want to poke. When Roth stung, he stung hard.

Refocusing on the table model, Garth said, "This shit is going to be spectacular. So when are we breaking ground?"

Alonso blew out a heavy sigh, the name Vivian Moore flashing in his head. "Still trying to tie up a few loose ends."

A hint of concern spread across Garth's face. "Is there a problem?"

"Nothing I can't handle." Alonso hoped Garth would drop the subject there, but of course it couldn't have been that simple.

"Is it with the last house you need to acquire? What happened to the letter you were going to send? That would definitely get the ball rolling for sure."

Alonso thought about the letter he'd written with the intent of sending it to the building code division. He retrieved the scathing correspondence from his drawer and studied his signature. A second later, he stuck it back inside. "I'll give her a chance to come to her senses before I force her hand. That's the gentlemanly thing to do." Plus, after spending time with Vivian, he wasn't sure this was the route he wanted to take any longer.

Garth barked a laugh. "Alonso Wright a gentleman?" He laughed again.

Alonso wasn't offended by the ridicule. Very few people truly knew him.

"Well, I know people. Say the word and I'll make sure it's declared uninhabitable. Then she'll have to sell. That bit—"

"Whoa," Alonso said, flashing his palms, a hint of unexplainable anger swelling inside of him at the idea of

Garth calling Vivian that word. Finding his calm, he said, "I got it handled."

"I hope so. This...*woman* is standing in the way of my money." Garth checked his watch. "I got a meeting to get to." He turned and started away. Stopping, he faced Alonso again. "You let me know if you need me to handle it. They don't call me the Problem Solver for nothing."

A smug Garth ambled away.

Alonso's grandfather used to say an overly confident man was dangerous and a man controlled by money was deadly. Lately, Garth had become both, which made him a liability Alonso didn't need. He already had enough problems. Namely, Vivian Moore. The seductive siren had whipped some kind of spell on him.

"Jesus Christ! This man just doesn't give up."

Vivian deleted the fifth voice mail message she'd received from Alonso Wright since their meeting two weeks ago. Hadn't he picked up on the fact she'd been avoiding his calls? Mainly because since their lunch she hadn't been able to stop thinking about the brash man.

So not good.

"Who?"

Vivian joined Tressa at the round table inside the nurses' lounge. "*Alonso Wright.* That real estate developer I told you about who is determined to purchase my grandmother's house. My house," she corrected.

Tressa bit into a carrot. "Don't companies like his usually have people who handle the grunt work? Are you sure the house is the only thing he's after?"

Vivian shot her a scowl. "Eat your rabbit food."

"Tell me again how you attempted to make a dramatic exit and forgot your purse." Tressa—her soon-to-be former best friend—laughed as if it'd been the funniest story she'd ever heard.

"Is that what friends do now? Laugh at each other's pain?"

"Aww. Come here." Tressa stood, rounded the table and draped her arms around Vivian's neck. "It's okay. We've all made fools of ourselves in front of men we like."

When Tressa burst into laughter again, Vivian shooed her away. "It's not funny. And I don't like him. At least, not in the way you're suggesting." *Like him. Please.* Tressa flashed her signature do-I-look-dumb-to-you expression. "Okay, maybe there's something about him I'm drawn to. But any woman would be drawn to him," she said in an attempt to downplay her attraction. Then it hit her. Had she really just admitted that aloud? And to the woman who'd been trying to play matchmaker for the last year.

"Obviously there's something about you he's drawn to, as well."

"Yeah, there is. It's called business. I have something he wants, remember?"

"Oh, you have something he wants all right and something tells me it has very little to do with business. Him brushing crumbs from your cheek. Calling to make sure you got home safe after your lunch meeting. Uh…that doesn't sound like any *business* practices I've ever heard of. Sounds personal to me. Really *personal*. Romantic, even. You two are like a happily-ever-after just waiting to happen."

Vivian glared at her starry-eyed friend. "You think that because you're a female Cupid. Always floating around shooting arrows in people's asses. Everything to you is romantic."

Tressa laughed. "Maybe. But you have to admit, it feels good to be chased, right? Gotta love a determined man."

"I'm not being chased, and this isn't determination. It's borderline harassment."

Tressa reached across and snagged one of Vivian's strawberries. "Are you attracted to him?"

"No."

"Bullshit. You're doing that thing."

That thing? Vivian's brow furrowed. "What thing?"

Tressa pointed to Vivian's hand. "That thing you do when you're lying or nervous. Tangling your fingers together."

Did she really? Vivian eased her hands into her lap. "Okay. Maybe a little." Tressa shot her a narrow-eyed gaze that screamed: *Liar, liar pants on fire.* Dammit. The woman could read her like a book. "Okay, okay. Maybe a lotta." She groaned. "But it doesn't matter. I'm not trying to reel him in. I'm trying to toss him back. Besides, he wants my house, not me."

"What if I'm right and he does want you? Then what?"

Vivian glanced away briefly. "I don't think I'll ever trust a man again. Not after…" Vivian refused to say the bastard's name. "I'm not willing to sacrifice any more pieces of myself, or my heart."

A somber expression spread across Tressa's face. "That lowlife you dated was just one row of sour grapes. Don't let his inability to be a man taint the entire vineyard. Who knows, this Alonso Wright could be the one you're destined to stomp grapes with."

Vivian burst out laughing. The serious expression on Tressa's face made her laugh even harder.

"I'm being serious here, Vi."

A failed attempt at composing herself earned Vivian a scowl from Tressa. "I know. I'm sorry. It's just that your analogies crack me up. So poetic, yet so…hilarious, at times."

Tressa dismissed her with a wave of the hand. "Anyway…"

"Can we talk about something other than my lacking

love life? Everyone can't be as blissfully happy as you and your dynamic fiancé."

A wide smile crept across Tressa's face as she eyed the engagement ring she'd recently been given. A small part of Vivian envied the happiness Tressa had found—even if she wasn't overly fond of her fiancé and thought Tressa might be moving just a little too fast. But a larger part was overjoyed for her. She deserved all the happiness she could handle. She was a good person, but more important, an amazing friend. Vivian cherished their relationship.

Tressa bit into another carrot. "Maybe you should consider selling, Vi."

Tressa's words snatched Vivian from her thoughts. Vivian shot Tressa a razor-sharp glance. Of all people, Tressa knew how much that house meant to her. "Excuse me?"

Tressa flashed her palms in mock surrender. "Before you slice me in half with that look of death, just hear me out. A year ago, I would have been the first to say let him take that three hundred thousand and stick it up his bleep." Tressa's tone softened. "But, sweetie, that was before Tyler—the spineless bastard—ran off with all the money you'd saved to renovate the place."

Tyler. Even thinking her ex's name boiled the blood in her veins. Her hand tightened into a fist as anger swelled inside her. How'd she ever fall for a con man like him? She answered a moment later. *Because I let my guard down.* And because of it, The Irma Moore House—named after her grandmother—she'd intended to open for homeless families had suffered.

Vivian's eyes lowered to the pimento cheese sandwich she no longer wanted. "Yeah, I've thought about it." *Many times.* But there was no better way to honor her Nina—a woman who'd given selflessly to others all of her life—than by converting the house she'd loved into something steeped in love.

Tressa touched her hand. "Vi, are you okay?"

Vivian glanced up, pasting a forced smile on her face. "Yeah, I'm good." She didn't care how much Alonso Wright offered her. She didn't want one red cent of his money. Wanting *him*…now, that was a different story.

"You should—"

Tressa's eyes went big. The expression on her face—a mix of surprise and caution—forced Vivian to turn to see what had her so stunned. The second her eyes landed on Alonso, her pulse quickened. What in the hell was he doing there?

Vivian's eyes raked the length of his lofty physique. The black T-shirt he wore revealed more of his chiseled frame than she'd seen during either of their previous encounters. The relaxed-fit jeans drew her attention to his lower half, which was just as impressive as the upper. Was there any piece of clothing he didn't look scrumptious wearing?

Finding his eyes—and her breath—she stood. "What are you doing here?"

He neared her, holding a bunch of fresh tulips. "You're ignoring me, and I wanted to know why." He shrugged. "So I thought I'd ask."

The closer he got the warmer the room grew. If he took one more step, she'd suffer heatstroke. "I—I'm not ignoring you. I just wasn't aware there was anything left to discuss." He flashed a half smile packed with so much sexiness and beautiful mischief she tingled all over.

"Um, I should get back on the floor."

Shit. With Alonso's presence, Vivian had forgotten Tressa was even in the room. His eyes lingered a moment more on Vivian before sliding to Tressa.

"Don't let me rush you off," he said.

"I have things to do." Tressa stuck out her hand. "I'm Tressa Washington. Vivian's best friend."

Alonso took Tressa's hand. "Alonso Wright. Nice to meet you."

"Nice to meet you, too. Do you believe in destiny?"

"Tressa!" Vivian forced through clenched teeth. When Alonso flashed her a quizzical expression, she sputtered a nervous laugh.

"I have to go." Tressa reclaimed her hand and disappeared from the room.

God, she was going to kill that woman.

Alonso chuckled. "She sure is interesting."

And a dead woman.

An awkward silence played between them. Alonso's eyes combed slowly over her face. When they lowered to her mouth, a bout of nerves shook her. In an effort to thwart the effects of his gaze, she said, "So…" Alonso's eyes jerked upward as if her words had startled him.

"These are for you. Tulips." He pushed the vibrant flowers toward her. "Your favorite."

Yes, they were, but how did he know tulips were her favorite? Was he stalking her? Apparently, he read the questioning on her face.

"I pay attention to details. It makes me good at what I do."

He captured her hand and flipped it palm-side up, then smoothed the pad of his thumb across the single red tulip tattooed on her wrist. The sensation of his warm touch and delicate stroke ignited her entire body. Her nipples beaded in her bra and she prayed it wasn't pronounced enough that Alonso would notice. She was afraid to look.

Reclaiming her hand, she said, "Thank you. They were my grandmother's favorite. Mine, too," she said as if he didn't already know that.

Again, Alonso scrutinized her as if committing her features to memory. He'd eyed her in a similar manner at the restaurant, too, she recalled. What exactly did he see when he stared at her that way?

"Why are you here?" she said, breaking the silence.

"Have dinner with me."

"Why would I do that?"

"Because you think I'm a nice guy."

"Actually, I don't think about you at all."

"Liar."

Vivian's brows bunched. "*Excuse* me?"

"The way your eyes smiled when you looked at me suggested you have thought about me." He shrugged. "At least once or twice."

"The way my eyes…" She laughed, attempting to strip away the nervousness that lingered just below the surface. "You are hilarious." He flashed one of those soul-stirring smiles. If that hadn't been enough, he performed that two-fingered beard massage thing that was quickly becoming her kryptonite. Why in the hell did she find the move so damn arousing?

Alonso folded his arms across his chest and rocked back and forth on his heels. "Well, I guess I was wrong."

"I'm sure that was hard for you to admit, being wrong, but it happens to the best of us." Oh, she would sacrifice a limb to know what raced through his head at the moment. The roguish expression on his face made the possibilities endless.

"About that dinner?"

He was a persistent one. She scrutinized him. *What kind of game are you playing, Alonso Wright?* Clearly, this was some elaborate scheme he'd cooked up in an attempt to persuade her to change her mind about selling the house. She'd played the fool once for a man, but wouldn't again. This time she would wield the upper hand and beat him at whatever diversion he'd crafted. "Okay."

Alonso's brow arched in what she took to be surprise.

Had he expected to have to put up more of a fight? He wasn't the only astonished one. Typically, she wasn't one to play games, but he made the challenge so damn appealing. Maybe she should have made him work a little harder.

"Okay?" Alonso said, his words dripping with uncertainty.

"Yes, okay. Unless you've already changed your mind." She mimicked his folded-arm stance. "You haven't changed your mind, have you?"

"Hell, no."

She bit back a smile. "Good."

"My best friend plays at a jazz club in downtown. The food is amazing. But we can do whatever you'd like."

What she'd like to do was definitely *not* an option. "I love jazz, actually."

"I know."

"How—"

He touched the charm bracelet she wore, grasping the sterling silver saxophone between his fingers. "Details."

She couldn't recall a man ever paying this much attention to detail. Her arms fell to her sides, not wanting to risk another wave of sensation like what had crashed through her earlier.

They spent the next few minutes making plans. The upcoming weekend was no good for either of them, so they scheduled for the following Friday.

Vivian checked her watch. "I really should get back to work."

"Okay. I have to get going, too. I'm getting Hamilton settled into his new place."

"That's great." Vivian thought back to the conversation she'd overheard between him and Hamilton. Hamilton hadn't sounded too interested, but apparently Alonso had changed his mind. If Alonso was that good at persuasion, maybe she should rethink this dinner thing. "How is Hamilton? No sodas, right?"

Alonso chuckled. "He's good. And no sodas."

She wasn't sure she believed him about the soda part. "That's good. That's really good." Things fell silent. What the hell was she doing? Why had she convinced herself any of this would be okay?

"Hey. You okay?"

Vivian snapped from her thoughts. Smiling, she said, "Yes. I was just thinking about how happy I am that Hamilton—" Her words trailed off seeing the wide grin on Alonso's face. "What?"

"Nothing."

"It's something. What?"

"I just like the way someone else's fortune brings you happiness. It's refreshing."

Something tender flashed in his eyes and for a brief moment, it blinded her to the fact she didn't fully trust his motives. "I just like seeing people make changes for the better. Tell Hamilton I said hello."

"Will do."

Alonso sauntered away, leaving his manly scent behind for Vivian to appreciate. If she had any sense at all, she'd run far, far away from the man, instead of sprinting toward him.

Chapter 5

Heavy rain pelleted Vivian's bedroom window, effects from the hurricane forming off the coast. This weather was unfit for anyone to venture out in. Her thoughts went to Hamilton. Thank God Alonso convinced him to get off the streets.

Unfortunately, Hamilton was only one of many. The thought of anyone suffering through this storm saddened her. What soothed her was the fact that the homeless had unique ways of braving the elements.

Lifting her cell phone from the nightstand, she scrolled through her contact list until coming to Alonso's name. They'd have to reschedule their evening. She didn't like driving in the rain, and even if she did, it would take an act of God to drag her from the dry comfort of her home.

A wave of disappointment washed over her as the phone rang in her ear. Had she actually been looking forward to spending an evening with Alonso? She groaned. Yes, she had. *All the more reason to cancel.*

Alonso answered on the fourth ring. At least she thought it was Alonso. The masculine voice on the opposite end was heavy. "Alonso?"

"Hey."

"You didn't sound like yourself."

"Sorry. I was on the treadmill. I'm a little winded."

An image of him bare chested and glistening played in her head. Shaking off the enticing visual, she refocused on the call. "Um, with the weather being so nasty, I think it's best if we reschedule. I don't drive—"

"I'll come to you. I really should be picking you up anyway, instead of you meeting me. That's the gentlemanly thing to do."

She'd suggested meeting him as a precaution. If by chance the night went horribly wrong, she'd have her own vehicle and could make a clean getaway. Him coming there? Probably not a good idea.

"Even better," he continued, "we don't have to go out at all. I can pick something up. What do you say?"

He seemed awfully determined to not allow her to cancel. Had he spent the past two weeks looking forward to this, too? The notion brought a hint of a smile to her lips. *Make a decision, Vivian. Yes or no.*

"Um…okay. Sure, that's fine." What was it about this man that forced her to push all rational thinking aside?

"Great. So…what would you like for me to pick up?"

"You're good with details. Surprise me."

"You should know I like a challenge. I'll see you soon."

They ended the call and Vivian collapsed onto the bed, pulled a pillow over her face and pretended to smother herself. "What have you gotten yourself into, Vivian Gayle Moore? You know you should have said no. Hell, no, to be precise."

Well, at least the night could be beneficial. Once Alonso discovered they had absolutely nothing in common, he'd vanish from her life. But what if they did have things in common? It didn't matter if they did. This wasn't a love connection, she reminded herself.

And how could they have anything in common? He'd probably never struggled a day in his life.

She'd struggled plenty.

He struck her as black-tie.

She was definitely casual Friday.

He was luxury.

She was... Well, she was luxury, too, but in a certified preowned type of way.

"Nope. Nothing at all in common."

Springing forward, she sat on the edge of the bed. One upside, she didn't have to get all dolled up to sit in her living room. "Jeans and a T-shirt it is."

Thunder cracked, followed by several fingers of lightning that lit her bedroom, then more thunder. "Jesus." When the lights flickered she went in search of candles. *Just in case.* She ignored the romantic value of a candlelit dinner with Alonso. "You are pathetic, Vivian Moore."

Two hours later, Vivian welcomed a drenched Alonso into her dimly lit home. "Good grief. You're soaked." As if he needed her to point that out to him. "Let me help you with those." She took two of the four bags he carried.

"It's awfully cozy in here. I like it."

"The storm knocked out the power. What is all of this?" she asked, setting the bags on the coffee table.

"Food from your favorite restaurant."

"My favorite rest—" Just then, she saw the Caliente Mexicana logo. "How did—" She stopped abruptly.

"Details," they said in unison.

Damn, he was good.

"You and the owner of the restaurant seemed familiar, so I assumed you frequented the place. And if you frequented the place, it must be your favorite. At least one of them."

"Do you pay this close attention to everyone you meet?" She laughed, but sobered when she noted the stern expression on Alonso's face.

"No, I don't."

Alonso's eyes lowered to her mouth, and a warm sensation blossomed in her stomach. "*Umm*…let's get you out of these wet clothes before you catch pneumonia." A corner of his mouth lifted into a roguish smile, and she shook her head. "Whatever outlandish thoughts are racing through that head of yours, stop them."

He shrugged. "What? I just like the idea of you…"

She narrowed her eyes at him.

"…wanting to keep me healthy. You thought I was going to say 'undressing me,' didn't you?"

"No."

"Yeah, right." He wagged his finger at her. "You should really get your mind out of the gutter."

Vivian bit back a smile, then sighed heavily for effect. "Follow me."

"Anywhere," Alonso said with a wink.

God, he was so full of it. As they moved down the hallway toward the laundry room, she envisioned peeling the wine-colored T-shirt from his soaking body, the heat of their desire causing the moisture on his chest to turn to steam. Then unbuttoning his jeans and inching them down his solid frame with unhurried anticipation.

"Earth to Vivian."

She turned to face him, slamming into the brick of his chest. "Oh." She stumbled a couple steps backward. Finding her equilibrium, she said, "I'm sorry. What did you say?"

"I asked how long the power has been out." A quizzical expression slid across his face. "Are…you okay?"

No, she wasn't, but nodded anyway. "Yes. Uh…about half an hour." She continued toward the laundry room. "I'm sure it'll be on any second now."

"That would be unfortunate," he said in a whisper.

She wasn't sure whether or not he'd intended her to hear him. Either way, she didn't respond. "Here we are. I'll step out while you—" Vivian gasped the second she turned, her eyes slamming into Alonso's finely sculpted bare chest.

Her eyes fixed on the display of all man in front of her. Smooth, chocolate, and a six-pack so defined that if she wasn't seeing it for herself, she'd never have believed the description. She wanted to touch him. Wanted to touch him so desperately her fingertips tingled, along with other parts. If she'd been brave enough—or insane enough—she'd have walked right up to him and glided her eager fingers over every rock-hard inch of him.

Her mouth went dry, then watered. Mesmerized, her eyes roamed over him—slowly, determinedly—like an inspector probing for damage. None that she could see. But then she saw the scar on his side. Her curiosity bloomed. It was a knife wound. Several years old, if she had to guess. How had he gotten it?

"Are you checking me out?"

Alonso's humor-filled words snatched her back to reality. "What? No, I'm not checking you out. *Psh.*"

"Liar."

Yes. Yes, she was a liar. And by the end of the night, this man would have her on the fast track to hell. "Don't flatter yourself. I've seen better chests on stick figures."

"Uh-huh. Well, I think I'll strip out of these pants, too. If that's okay?"

His pants? Alarm settled into the pit of her stomach. "Wh-wh-what?"

"Don't look so stunned. I'm only kidding."

Vivian released a sound that was somewhere between a laugh, a chuckle and a plea for help.

"But for the record, I'm not bashful," Alonso said.

Vivian folded her arms across her chest, struggling to keep her eyes pinned to his. "I imagine no woman has ever tossed you out in the pouring rain before."

He smoothed two fingers along his jawline. *Quit that*, she inwardly scorned. A sexy chuckle floated past his lips as he flashed a palm in surrender. Vivian didn't celebrate the win, because it would probably be the only battle she won all night.

Chapter 6

Finished with their meal, Alonso stretched his legs out to their full length on the carpeted floor. Instead of enjoying their meal in the kitchen, they'd set up buffet-style on the coffee table, eaten by candlelight and listened to old-school R & B on his cell phone.

God, he was stuffed, which only made the two-sizes-too-small T-shirt Vivian had practically forced over his head that much more uncomfortable. And not to mention the sweatpants that had a death grip on his balls.

In hindsight, maybe he should have kept on his drenched pants, instead of deciding at the last minute they should be laid out to dry, too.

Normally, he would have never stepped into another man's clothes, but he hadn't wanted to appear ungrateful. Plus, he doubted Vivian could handle him sitting around in his birthday suit. Especially if the way she'd reacted to seeing him bare chested was any indication. Her eyes had fixed on the scar decorating his side. He was surprised she hadn't asked about it.

"Was your ex a gnome? I think this shirt is cutting off my circulation."

"He definitely wasn't built as sturdily as you."

By the stunned expression on her face, he gathered she regretted allowing the words to slip past her lips. But why? He wasn't oblivious to her attraction to him. And the feeling was definitely mutual.

"What happened between you two, if you don't mind me asking?" Vivian's jaw tightened, then relaxed. If he had to guess, they hadn't ended things on good terms. "You don't have to answer that." Though he hoped she would. Her reaction to the question piqued his curiosity.

Had they grown apart? Had he cheated on her? Had she cheated on him? The latter seemed less likely. She didn't strike him as the unfaithful type. He'd always been good at reading people. Especially women.

"He stole from me."

Alonso assumed she meant money. What kind of coward stole from his woman? More questions came. Had the lowlife been jobless, living off Vivian? On drugs and in need of a fix?

Vivian didn't elaborate. Instead she sipped her wine and stared at the flickering candle flame. Observing her sadness, Alonso regretted making her revisit an apparently still-raw subject.

"His loss is another man's gain, right?" The words had been meant to soothe her, but something told him he'd missed the mark.

"Alonso…" She paused. "I'm sure your charms work on most of the women you unleash them on, but I'm not one of them. This—" she fanned her hand over the spread of food "—all of this." Her hands moved between them. "It doesn't get you any closer to what you want."

"Huh." He took a sip from his glass. "Tell me again what exactly it is you think I want."

"My house."

"Oh. Okay."

Her eyes lit with questions her mouth didn't ask. No doubt his cryptic response had confused her and possibly intrigued her, too. *Good.* "So, how'd I do? With dinner, I mean."

It took her a minute to answer, the perplexed expression melting from her face. "Like you said, it's my favorite restaurant."

He wanted to let Vivian's earlier comment go, but for some reason it gnawed at him. Shifting toward her, he said, "You do know that two people can enjoy a meal together without one wanting something from the other, right?"

"Yes. But I also know people rarely do anything without wanting or expecting something in return."

Well, he couldn't argue with that. "Tonight, this moment, I want absolutely nothing from you. A meal is just a meal. No strings attached."

This time he was the liar, because he did want something from her, in the worst way imaginable. He wanted to crush his mouth against those beautiful lips he'd fantasized about all night. He wanted to drag his tongue down the length of her torso, making her shiver with anticipation. He wanted to stare into those mesmerizing eyes as he pushed deep inside of her. Wanted to hear her cry out in ecstasy.

Vivian tilted her head to the side and eyed him. It took everything inside of him to not lean forward and capture her mouth.

"We'll see," she finally said.

Why did he get the feeling he'd been defeated but just didn't know it yet?

"Would you like some coffee?"

Vivian's words drew him away from his paralyzing thoughts. "No. I hate coffee. Yuck."

She pushed her fingertips into her chest. "You don't like coffee? Oh, we can't be friends."

They shared a bout of much-needed laughter. Things took on a more relaxed tone.

Alonso bent one knee. "When I was ten, I thought I was the man."

"Like now?"

They shared another round of laughter.

"I'm sorry. Go on," she said.

"Like I was saying before I was rudely interrupted…" He bumped her playfully. "I took a huge swig from my grandfather's mug. Ten seconds after I swallowed the tar, I threw up all over the kitchen floor. I haven't touched the stuff since."

"Ah. Now it makes sense. Well, for my sixteenth birthday, my grandmother gave me my very own old-school percolator. My mother was not happy. She didn't like the idea of me drinking coffee. But who argues with grandparents?"

"No one," he said, his thoughts shifting to his grandfather.

"I remember at my sweet sixteen party I made all of my friends coffee to go along with their cake. Most of them were like you and hated it. But I think that's because I wasn't as good at making it then as I am now."

"Yeah, I'm sure that was it."

"When my grandmother passed, I never used the percolator again."

"Why?"

She shrugged. "I don't know. Too many memories, I guess. I still have it packed away somewhere."

"Maybe one day you'll use it to brew me a cup."

"You don't touch the stuff, remember?"

"For you, I'd make the sacrifice."

Vivian placed her glass on the table. "I bet you had a huge shindig and got a brand-spanking-new car for your sixteenth birthday."

"No and no. I didn't get a new car until I was around twenty-six. And I've never had a birthday party."

A look of shock spread across Vivian's face. "You've never had a birthday party? Not even as a child?"

He shook his head. "I almost had one when I was eight."

Her brows furrowed. "Almost? How do you almost have a birthday party?"

Alonso eyed her long and hard, debating whether or not to share one of the most painful days of his life with her. To be honest, he couldn't believe he was even considering it at all. *What is it about you, Vivian Moore?*

He slid his gaze away and studied the flame of the candle. "My mother went to the store to get stuff for my party that was supposed to have been the next weekend. I was so excited. My very first birthday party."

Alonso silently recalled how he hadn't been able to sleep just thinking about the impending event. "One hour passed. Two hours passed. No mom. Three days later I called my grandfather to come and get me. There was no more food left in the house, and the gas had just been shut off. It was February, so it was freezing."

"You were alone for three days? At eight years old?"

"I was used to taking care of myself."

"What happened to your mom? Was she okay?"

Alonso's stare fixed on the flickering candle. Why had he thought talking about this would be a good idea? "It was like she dropped off the face of the earth. Of course, I thought she had to be dead for her not to come for me. A few weeks later, I'm in the corner store and she walks in. I'd been so pissed at her, but that anger faded the second I saw her. Her clothes were tattered. She looked as if she hadn't slept in days. She smelled like the gutter. Still, she was the most beautiful woman in the world to me."

When Vivian swallowed hard, he could tell she was fighting back her own emotions.

"I rushed to her, 'Mom, Mom,' and draped my arms around her thin frame." He lowered his head. "This woman… The woman I'd loved unconditionally for my entire life shoved me away, looked me dead in my eyes and said, 'Who the hell are you?' It. Crushed. Me."

"Oh, my God."

All of the pain he'd felt that day came rushing back like water from a flushing fire hydrant. "It was the last time I ever saw her." Alive. He'd attended her funeral six months later.

When he faced Vivian, tears streamed down her face. "Shit. I didn't mean to make you cry." She flinched when he touched her silky skin, but didn't pull away as he glided the pad of his thumb across her cheek.

Vivian swiped her hand across her opposite cheek. "I'm a big softy sometimes." The lights flashed on and she jerked, placing her hand over her heart. "Jesus. That scared me. I'll toss your clothes in the dryer for a few minutes."

Vivian appeared refreshed when she returned a few minutes later. Obviously she'd used the dryer as an excuse to get herself together. Pushing to his feet, Alonso said, "It's late. I better get out of here. You probably need your rest for work tomorrow."

"Actually, I'm on vacation for the next twelve days."

Was that her way of asking him to stay longer? Could it mean she wanted to spend more time with him? Any more time with this woman would get him in real trouble. Ignoring the possible implications, he said, "Twelve days, huh? Big plans?"

"Sleep."

He nodded. Being a nurse had to be exhausting. Plus

she seemed to give so much of herself to her patients. Why couldn't he stop staring at her? Even without her face plastered with makeup—which he appreciated because she didn't need it—she was a thing of pure beauty.

Silence fell between them. It was obvious they were both reaching for something to say. Their gazes held, snatching him deeper into her world with each breath. He wasn't sure what—if anything—his gaze did to her, but the longer their connection held the more anxious she appeared.

Finally, Vivian interrupted the harmony of their unspoken thoughts. Pointing over her shoulder, she said, "You remember how to get to the laundry room, right?"

He chuckled. "My memory is not that bad yet."

By the time he'd made his way to the laundry room, re-dressed in his own clothes and returned to the living room, Vivian had cleared the table, packed the food and placed it back in the bags.

"This will make great leftovers," she said, offering Alonso the bounty.

He flashed his palm. "No, you keep them. I'm not much for leftovers. This will just sit in the fridge until it turns green and fuzzy."

"Eww."

"The life of a bachelor."

She did that head-tilt thing, folded her arms across her chest and studied him. "That's hard to believe."

"What, that I don't do leftovers?"

"That you're single. What's wrong with you?"

Her brazen manner excited him. "What's wrong with me? Why does something have to be wrong with me?"

Before she could answer, the lights flicked off again.

Vivian groaned. "Come on, not again."

Obviously, the universe felt sympathy for her because, a second later, they flashed on again.

Intentionally skating around her earlier question, he said,

"I better get out of here." There was something wrong with him—betrayal had hardened him. But he'd given her too much of a glimpse inside of him already to offer her more.

Vivian nodded. "Okay. I…had a good time tonight, Alonso."

"Did you doubt you would?"

She shrugged. "Could have gone either way, I guess." A sly smile curled her lips.

"Good night, Vivian Moore."

"Good night, Alonso Wright."

When he turned to leave, Vivian gasped, then yanked at the hem of his shirt. He pivoted. "What's wrong?"

She shook her head with urgency. "Nothing."

He noted her guilt-ridden expression and hand behind her back. "What are you hiding?"

She held up her free hand. "Nothing."

Nothing had become her theme. "Let me see your other hand."

Vivian placed the free hand she'd shown him behind her back again and flashed him the opposite one. Alonso barked a laugh. What was this woman up to? In a bold move, he hooked his arm around her waist, pulled her to him and attempted to retrieve whatever she was hiding.

Her laughter filled the room. The sweet, joyful sound swelled his chest. Hearing her laughter was far better than seeing her in tears. After a moment or two of tussling, the tightening inside his boxers gave him a stern warning to pull away, which he did.

Instead of Vivian following his lead, she leaned in and pressed her lips against his in a gentle peck that hadn't lasted nearly long enough.

Vivian's eyes widened and she slapped her hand over her mouth, a pair of silky, royal blue panties sandwiched between. So that's what she'd been hiding. They'd apparently been stuck to his shirt.

Dropping her hand and placing it behind her back again, she said, "Oh, God... I'm so s—"

Before she finished the unnecessary apology, he covered her mouth with his. She tensed in his arms, but melted into his chest a second later. His tongue danced in perfect accord with hers. His hands slid along her rib cage, then wrapped around her in a possessive embrace.

Her mouth tasted delicious, the sweetness of the wine she sipped lingering on her lips. Greed overtook him and he did his best to consume her whole. Vivian's moans further stirred his hunger. All he could think about was stripping the clothes from her body, easing her to the carpeted floor and burying himself as deep inside of her as he could get.

If he hadn't been wearing underwear, he was sure he'd have an imprint of his zipper on his dick. Hands down, this was the best kiss he'd ever experienced. And if kisses had the ability to impregnate, she'd have definitely been pregnant with triplets.

Just as quickly as the kiss had started, Vivian ended it with the same sense of urgency, pulling away as if they were teenagers who'd been caught by her overprotective father. Staring into her vulnerable eyes, he didn't question or protest her actions, despite wanting to. She'd had a reason for pulling away, and he respected that.

Alonso brushed a bent finger along her cheek, turned and left.

Thirty minutes later, he pulled into his driveway. He allowed his head to crash back against the headrest, a heavy sigh escaping. "You shouldn't have kissed her, Wright." As if he'd had the power to resist. "Shit." This complicated things.

His cell phone chimed and he fished it from the center console. The text icon flashed in the center of his screen. Tapping it twice, a message from Vivian appeared:

Just checking to make sure you made it home safely.

An umbrella punctuated the sentence. He was glad she texted in proper English. Trying to decipher some of the texts he received often gave him a headache.

It was rough but made it!

He located an image of a boat and inserted it before hitting Send.

Good. I enjoyed tonight. Thank you.

Me, too. And no need for thanks.

A smiley face preceded her next message.

Sweet dreams.

You, too.

Just as he reached for the door handle, another text came through.

The kiss was nice.

Yes, it was.

How did he reply? Did he reveal that for those exhilarating seconds their lips were locked he felt as if he were flying? Or did he confess he'd wanted her so badly his hands had shaken? How about telling her no woman had ever affected him, confused him, consumed him like she had in such a short period of time?

Hell, no. He couldn't tell her any of those things. Instead, he replied with...nothing at all.

Chapter 7

Vivian hadn't expected Alonso to confess that the kiss they'd shared had been the best kiss he'd ever had, but she'd at least expected some type of response. What had she gotten? Nothing but radio silence for the past two days. Served her right. How in the hell did she go from considering him the Antichrist to sucking face with him? She blamed sexual deficiency.

She'd sparred with herself about even sending the stupid text. Why hadn't she followed her first instinct and not addressed it at all?

Because she'd felt she needed to say something.

Vivian touched two fingers to her lips. Although it'd been days since he'd kissed her, she could still feel the sensation of his lips against hers. She'd been kissed before, but what Alonso had done to her mouth defied description. *No words could capture that experience.* The way he'd held her close to him, the depth of the kiss...

Ugh. She shook her head to scatter the menacing

thoughts. There were far more important things that needed her attention than Alonso Wright. She eyed the rickety house in front of her. *Far more important things.*

A long while passed before she exited her vehicle and trudged toward 1411 Sycamore Place, her childhood home. It felt like ages since she'd been there. And when she thought about it, it had been. Eight months at least. Coming there reminded her that she'd failed.

Figuring the general contractor would arrive soon, she entered for a quick look around. She'd contacted Leon Johnson after receiving the notice from the city this morning that, loosely translated, read: make improvements or else.

The warning couldn't have come at a worse time. *Like I need one more complication.* Impediments were starting to become the theme for her life. *Don't dwell on the bad, focus on the good.* Hearing her grandmother's words in her head put a lazy smile on her face. *Yes, ma'am.*

The warped wood creaked under her feet as she made her way into the living room. Instantly, memories suffocated her. Her attention slid to a spot in front of the window. Every Christmas there stood an ornately decorated tree. Dozens of lights, homemade ornaments and stringed popcorn that she and her grandmother had microwaved the night before. And gifts. They weren't extravagant, but there were plenty.

When her chest tightened she shifted her focus to the four indentions in the tattered carpet where the baby grand piano once stood. Her grandmother had provided free lessons to the neighborhood kids. Vivian had donated the instrument after her death.

She closed her eyes and swayed to a melody she could only hear in her head. Stevie Wonder's "Ribbon in the Sky." A smile touched her lips, remembering how much Irma Moore had loved playing the piano, and that song.

After a few more soothing notes, Vivian made her way into the kitchen. The once-white linoleum was now a dingy cream color, curled at the edges and cracked by time. A strong odor of mildew lingered. She prayed the place didn't have a leak.

Moving farther into the house, she bypassed the stairs that led to the upper level and headed toward the room that held the most significant memories. When she turned the knob to what was once her grandmother's bedroom, it came off in her hand.

Well, at least the door itself is still intact.

As if the universe wanted to demonstrate its sense of humor, the door came crashing down the second she attempted to push it open.

How in the hell does a house deteriorate to this level so fast?

There was no one but herself to blame for the state of disarray here. This was all her fault. All of it. She should have never stopped coming by and checking on the place. But after that bastard ran off with the money... *No excuses*, she told herself.

Holding on to her diminishing cheery disposition, she stepped over the door and entered. Despite it being a sunny eighty-six degrees outside, the room was cold and dreary. Maybe that's what death did to a room—siphoned all warmth.

Standing by the bed where she'd held her grandmother's hand and watched as she'd taken her last breath, her eyes burned. "Fuck cancer," she said under her breath. "Fuck cancer," she repeated, this time only louder.

"Fuck it to the darkest depths of hell where it and all of its disciples belong."

Vivian turned urgently to see Leon standing behind her. She swiped at her eyes. "Leon? I'm sorry. I didn't hear you come in." Which surprised her, since every floorboard in the place appeared rotten.

Leon had done work for both her and her grandmother for years, so she trusted he wouldn't price gouge her on the estimate to bring the place up to code. If the man gave up home renovating, he would have no problem scoring a gig walking the runway. But as handsome as he was, he had nothing on her Alonso.

Her Alonso? Had she really just thought *her* Alonso?

"You seemed to be having a moment. I didn't want to disturb you. But when you damned cancer, I couldn't resist chiming in and condemning the bastard, too."

Vivian laughed. "Thanks for the support."

"I'm doing a 5K cancer run in a few weeks in honor of my mother, sister and aunt. You should join me."

Remembering what Leon had been through, Vivian felt overwhelming sympathy for him. To lose three family members to breast cancer, and within a few years, had to be tough. "Ha! I'd make it about twenty feet before I dropped face-first onto the concrete. I'm definitely not a runner."

"You sound like my girl."

They both laughed.

"So do you think I'll have to auction off a body part to pay for all of this?"

"Are you wanting to do just enough to appease the city or you are looking to do a full renovation?"

A complete overhaul of the house was her dream; unfortunately, that wasn't in the budget right now. "Just enough to avoid the 'or else' portion of the letter."

"Gotcha. I see all the other houses on the block have been snatched up by Wright Developing. Are you thinking about selling, too?"

At this point, maybe she should have been thinking about it. "No. I think I'm going to hold on to it." Trying to appear as nonchalant as possible, she asked, "What do you know about this Wright Developing?"

"Not much. Only what I've heard in passing."

"Which is?" So much for nonchalant.

"That the owner, Alonso, I believe is his name, is one hell of a businessman and a force to be reckoned with." Leon chuckled. "Which is why I'm surprised a Wright Developing sign isn't staked in your yard, too."

Well, she was also a force to be reckoned with. "Oh, trust me, he's tried."

"Huh. Well, that might explain the notice you received."

Her brows furrowed. "What do you mean?"

"The city doesn't usually get involved unless someone has launched a complaint. If Wright Developing is trying to get your property, odds are… You'd be amazed at the lengths some developers will go to get what they want."

Was it plausible? Would Alonso stoop to that level? A thousand questions plagued her and she wanted answers. And she knew just where to get them.

"Two days?" Roth barked a laugh. "You tell me you kissed this woman, it was the best kiss you've ever experienced, she sends you a text about the kiss and instead of responding, you give her the cold treatment for two days? Man, this woman really has you upside down."

Alonso wore a trail in the carpet pacing back and forth. He ran his hands over his head. "What in the hell do you think I've been trying to tell you? She's worked some kind of damn voodoo or something on me. I think about her morning, noon and night. It's like a damn sickness."

Roth relaxed back against the chair, then crossed his ankle over his knee. "I like her and I haven't even met her yet."

Alonso shot Roth a scowl and Roth flashed his palms in mock surrender.

Alonso drew his hands to his waist. "This shit doesn't happen to me. Did I tell you she tried to cancel our date this past Friday and I damn near begged her not to? I wanted to see her that bad." He stopped, tossed his head back and grunted a sound of pure pain. "Shit. Shit. Shit."

"It all makes sense now. You're afraid of her."

Alonso whipped his head toward Roth so fast he was surprised it didn't spring off his shoulders. "Afr— *Psh.* That's laughable."

"It may be laughable—" Roth studied him with a narrow-eyed gaze "—but it's true. You're afraid of this woman. Why?"

The only problem with his best friend: sometimes the man knew him better than he knew himself. Defeated, Alonso propped himself against the edge of his desk, crossed his arms over his chest and dipped his head. As much as he hated to admit it, maybe Roth was right. Maybe he was afraid of Vivian. Afraid of the thoughts that always included her. Afraid of how comfortable he was talking to her. Afraid of the way she made him feel when he was with her.

Alonso shrugged. "You're right." He lifted his head to eye Roth. "You. Are. Right. I'm afraid." Damn. Had he just admitted that out loud?

Before Roth could respond, Alonso's assistant's voice boomed over the speaker. "Mr. Wright, there's a Vivian Moore here to see you."

Alonso's brow arched. What was Vivian doing there?

"Looks like I'll finally get to meet the woman who has you completely whipped."

Alonso shot Roth the bird. "Send her in, Jessica." He pushed from his desk and ironed a hand down his shirt.

"You look fine, man," Roth joked.

The second Vivian entered his office, Alonso knew something was wrong. That warm and welcoming expression she normally wore was now a mix of disappointment and anger. Was she upset he hadn't called her? "Hey," he said, approaching her.

"May I speak with you a moment?" Her gaze cut briefly to Roth. "In private."

Uh-oh.

On cue, Roth stood. "I'll wait for you out front."

Any other time Alonso would have taken the opportunity to introduce the two, but Vivian didn't appear to be much into being cordial at the moment. When the door clicked shut, Alonso directed Vivian to the chair Roth had occupied.

"I'm not interested in sitting, Alonso." She snatched something from her purse and shoved it toward him. "Did you have something to do with this?"

Alonso accepted the paper. City of Raleigh was printed across the top, along with the word NOTICE in red block letters. After skimming the contents, he groaned to himself. Although he had nothing to do with this, he still felt guilty, because he had a pretty good idea of who was responsible. *Garth.* "You really think I have something to do with this?"

"I was told that's what you developers do. He also said when they don't get what they want they resort to these types of underhanded tactics."

He? At that moment, the mystery *he* became the urgent part of the conversation. Who was *he*, and how did *he* fit into Vivian's life? What was Alonso worried about? No way could they be romantically involved, right?

Nah. If they were, Vivian would have never spent an evening with him. And she certainly wouldn't have stuck her tongue down his throat. A hint of calm—and relief—settled over him.

Refocusing on the conversation, he said, "*He* was right. That is a tactic used by some developers." He shook his head and waved the paper in the air. "But not me. I don't have to get down and dirty like this." But he had in the past.

"Sure."

Vivian snatched the paper from his hand, the crisp, sharp edge slicing into his hand. "Ahh, shit." A trickle of blood rolled along his palm. "Shit."

Vivian's eyes widened and her hardened expression turned to one of urgent concern. She dropped the paper and her purse to the floor and captured his hand. "Oh, God. I'm so sorry."

"Who would have guessed you were so abusive?" When her apologetic eyes rose to meet his, all he wanted to do was yank her into his arms and kiss the hell out of her. And this time, there would be no pulling away.

"Do you have a first aid kit?"

He head nodded toward his personal facilities. "In the bathroom."

Vivian led him across the room, holding his hand as if he'd severed several fingers instead of suffering a minor paper cut. When they entered, the motion-activated lights lit the room.

"Wow, this is nicer than my master bath," she said.

He couldn't confirm or deny that claim…yet.

Alonso leaned against the edge of the marble countertop while Vivian scoured the first aid kit. While she worked on his wound, he watched her, studied her, fell deeper into her alluring web.

Without looking up, she said, "What?"

Alonso snapped out of his trance. "What, what?"

"I can feel your eyes on me."

He gave a slight head shake. "Nothing." She couldn't handle what was racing through his mind. "You like helping people."

"Was that a question?"

"No, an observation."

Her eyes met his, but only for a second. "Yes, I do."

"Why?"

She donned a confused expression when she brought her gaze up again. "Why, what?"

"Why do you like helping people?"

"Do I really need a reason to help someone?"

"No, I guess not. Why are you helping me? Especially when five minutes ago you looked as if you wanted to gut me and leave me in the woods for wild animals to feast on."

"So dramatic." She swiped at his injury. "I'm helping you because you're bleeding." Her tone lowered. "And… it's kinda my fault."

He barked a laugh. "Kinda?"

"Okay, okay, all my fault."

When Alonso brushed a hair from her face, she tensed. "Sorry. I gotta learn to keep my hands to myself." With Vivian, he deemed it an impossible feat.

"My Nina—grandmother—used to always tell me we had two hands for a reason. One to help ourselves, and one to help others. I help people because it makes me feel good. I help people because it's what I was taught. I help people because it's the right thing to do."

The qualities this woman possessed were just as attractive as her beautiful face and body. He guided his thoughts away from the sinful things he wanted to do to her. "So, how many stitches am I going to need, Nurse Vivian?" Vivian's laughter was truly one of the most glorious sounds he'd ever heard.

"Men."

With a Q-tip, she smoothed antiseptic cream on his cut. Her touch was gentle. Just what he'd expect from her. How would her touch be while they made love? Would her hands grip his biceps as he drove deep inside her? Or maybe glide along his sweat-slickened back as he brought her to a climax.

Oh, the possibilities. I've never met a woman like you, Vivian Moore. "The kiss was nice."

She paused a moment, but recovered quickly. "It was a mistake."

A mistake? Was she serious? "It didn't feel like a mistake." He eyed her, intently waiting for a response.

Finally, her eyes settled on him. "It was, and I owe you an apology."

"I don't accept it."

"Well, that is your right. All done." She collected the trash and tossed it into the basket.

"Have dinner with me again."

"No."

Damn. She could have acted as if she'd at least given it a second of thought. "No? Why?"

"I'm busy."

He laughed. "We haven't even discussed a day, so how do you know you're busy?"

Vivian exited the bathroom with Alonso on her heels. When she stopped—abruptly—he nearly collided into her. Clearly, she'd just now noticed the 3-D display. But her eyes didn't linger on it long. Instead, they moved to the view outside his window—the unobstructed view of her old neighborhood. Taking a step or two closer, she stared out as if in a trance.

"I have to go," she said, backing away. Collecting her purse and the letter, she hurried to the door.

Alonso rushed past her and blocked her escape. "What is it, Vivian? What about me spooks you?"

She placed her hand against his chest, then reclaimed it quickly. "Please move."

"Why—"

"Because I don't trust you, Alonso." Her tone lowered to almost a whisper. "I don't trust you."

"You don't trust me now, but you will. I guarantee it."

Alonso stepped aside and allowed her to run from him. He didn't intend on letting her get too far.

Chapter 8

Vivian homed in on the local news and their special coverage of the hurricane that had hit the coast and the devastation it'd left behind. Millions of dollars in property damage, flooding, power outages. Thankfully, there had been no loss of life. Her heart went out to all affected.

Raleigh had gotten rain and high winds. The wind had caused some damage, but they'd fared much better than their counterparts two hours east.

A call for volunteers scrolled across the bottom of the screen. *I should go.* She didn't have to return to work for another week and a half. *Why not?* She needed something to take her mind off Alonso. No man had ever gotten her the way he had.

Shaking off the thoughts of him, she lifted the cordless phone from the table. Before she could place the call to the help line, the doorbell rang. "Well, it's about time."

Tressa should have been here two hours ago. Vivian doubted her tardiness was her fault. *Cyrus.* Vivian wanted so badly to tell her friend she didn't believe Cyrus was the man for her and that she definitely shouldn't marry him after only a few months of dating, but was it really her place?

The part of Vivian that loved Tressa like a blood sister said yes. The part that was finally seeing Tressa happy urged her to tend to her own damn business. The more mindful part asked the question: *Who are you to judge?* She certainly wasn't the authority on men. She allowed a man to run off with her life savings and another to scramble her thoughts.

Vivian just prayed that the not-so-good feeling she had about Cyrus was just her being an overprotective friend and nothing more. Pulling open the door, she said, "Well, it's about—" The smile slid from her face, and she swallowed her unsaid words.

Alonso's domineering presence slammed into her like an unmanned train, taking her breath away. Several seconds of gawking at him foolishly passed. Finally rediscovering her voice, she said, "Alonso...?" That was all that would come out.

They hadn't spoken to each other since she'd visited his office the day before. The cordial thing to do would have been to invite him inside. But the lustful demon crawling just under the surface of her skin suggested inviting him in was probably a bad idea.

Ultimately, good upbringing won out. But she vowed to keep a safe distance between them. Stepping aside, she made a sweeping motion with her hand. "Come in."

When he strolled past, the scent of his cologne teased and paralyzed her all at the same time. *God, you smell amazing.* A quick reel of the last time he'd been there played in her head. Two fingers pressed against her lips as she recalled how perfect his mouth felt against hers. *Focus, Vivian. Focus.*

When Alonso rotated to face her, she jolted and dropped her hand. A look of confusion flashed across his face, but faded just as quickly. Cradling herself in her arms, she tilted her head and steadied a questioning gaze on him. "What are you doing here, Alonso?"

Alonso's eyes slid along her neck and she swore she could feel his touch. A wave of nervousness crashed through her. This man knew how to wreak havoc on her body. His daunting eyes resettled on hers and her breathing grew unsteady.

"I apologize for stopping by unannounced." His focus slid past her to the door. "You were expecting someone else?"

Of course she was. She was expecting anyone but him. "Yes."

"Ah." He slid his hands into his pockets. "A date?"

"Yes." It wasn't a complete lie. Maybe a mislead, but not a lie.

"Hmm."

She hadn't missed the moment his jaw tightened, then relaxed. Did the idea of another man entertaining her somehow trouble him? If so, why? There was definitely nothing between them. Heck, they weren't even friends.

"Anyway. My hand… I think it's infected."

Was he serious? The cut hadn't been any bigger than an eyelash. "And you chose to come here, rather than your physician's office?"

"Considering you're the one who maimed me—"

"Maimed?" She barked a laugh. "I've seen toddlers with more severe knee scrapes who didn't make as much of a fuss as you." Vivian wasn't oblivious to what he was trying to do, but she went along with his game. Holding out her hand, she said, "Let me see."

"Ouch. Are you trying to hurt my feelings?"

"I seriously doubt you bruise so easily."

Alonso chuckled that dizzying sound and offered his hand. For someone who sat behind a desk all day, he had the hands of a workingman. Not overly rough, but his hands weren't as soft as she'd assumed a man in his position would have.

"So, what do you think, Nurse Moore?"

She released his hand. "I think you're full of it. There's nothing wrong with your hand. But of course you knew that already."

He flashed a wicked smile. "Okay, I confess. It may have been a ploy."

"I don't like games, Alonso."

"Neither do I."

The pointed expression on his face rattled her. Obviously his words had been directed at her. A hard silence fell between them. She truly wanted to dislike this man. Not because he was a horrible person, but because she could see herself actually liking him.

"Come away with me."

Alonso's words banged her back to reality with a brutal jar. "Excuse me?"

"Come away with me. To the—"

Yeah, she thought that was what he said. "Why would I do that?"

"What better way to build trust than a road trip to hel—"

"Ha. You and I both know that's not a good idea."

Alonso folded his arms across his chest and narrowed her eyes at him. "Really? Why?"

Why? Was this his attempt at getting her to admit her attraction to him? Not. Gonna. Happen. "Because… Just because."

"*Ahh.* That trust thing you mentioned in my office. Let me ask you something." He rubbed two fingers along his jaw. "Is it *me* you don't trust…or yourself?"

The questions angered her. A true sign of guilt. "I—" Before she could finish her thought, the doorbell rang. Her feet remained rooted to the floor. The doorbell rang again, followed by several knocks.

"You should probably get that. You shouldn't keep him waiting. Not all men like that."

Vivian rolled her eyes as she moved away from Alonso to go to the door.

Tressa barreled in. "Whose Maserati is that in—" She paused when she spotted Alonso. "Oh."

A slow smile crept across Tressa's face and Vivian could just read the woman's mind. Vivian stood by the door. "Thank you for stopping by, Alonso."

"You're not leaving, are you?" Tressa asked. "You should come to lunch with us."

What the... Oh, she was going to strangle Tressa.

"Thanks for the invitation, but I have some things to take care of before I head to the coast."

Fine lines etched in Tressa's forehead. Vivian had to admit she was curious, too, since she'd just heard about the damage there. Surely he wasn't going to scout possible properties to purchase at a time like this.

"The coast?" Tressa asked, taking the words out of Vivian's mouth. "I hear it's bad there."

"I'm volunteering. Figured I could put my skills to good use."

"Wow. Good-looking and kindhearted. Isn't that something, Vivian?"

Oh, you are a dead woman. "Yep. Something."

"That sounds right up Vi's alley. I'm sure she'd love to go. Put her skills to good use, too."

"Actually, I invited her." Alonso glanced in Vivian's direction. "But she declined."

So the coast was the *come away with me* he'd meant. Why had he made it sound like he'd wanted to whisk her away to some exotic island? Or maybe that's just what she'd heard.

Tressa rested her hands on her hips. "Really?"

Alonso and Tressa stared at Vivian as if she'd committed an unforgivable atrocity and was about to be staked for it. "Thank you for stopping by, Alonso."

He chuckled, then smoothed his palm across his cheek. Removing his wallet, he fished inside and passed a hundred-dollar bill to Tressa. "You ladies enjoy your lunch date."

Vivian snatched the note from Tressa and shoved it back to Alonso. "Thank you, but no thank you."

Alonso eyed her but remained silent. If she had to guess, there was plenty he wanted to say. Luckily, he simply accepted the bill, smiled and strolled past her. Vivian didn't realize she'd been holding her breath until the door clicked shut.

"*Oh. My. Sweet. Jesus.* You two should come with a label—beware of flames. The chemistry between the two of you is off the freaking chart. When he looks at you, there's nothing but raw desire in his eyes. So please tell me why in the hell you just let that fine-ass man get away. You should have told him you'd travel with him to the damn moon and back."

Couldn't Tressa have at least given her a moment to recover?

"Are you listening to me, Vi?"

"Yes. Yes, I'm listening," she said in a less-than-enthusiastic tone.

"Then please tell me what the problem is."

The problem had just waltzed out the front door. Instead, she said, "There is no problem."

"Good. So…that means you're going to call Alonso and tell him you changed your mind about the trip, right?"

It wasn't that she didn't want to go; it was that she wanted to go far more than she would ever admit. "I wouldn't hold my breath."

* * *

Several hours had passed since he'd left Vivian's place, but the woman still lingered in his thoughts. His grandfather once told him he'd know he'd found the one when he couldn't think about anything else but her. Alonso couldn't say whether or not Vivian was "the one," but she surely wasn't giving up any real estate in his head.

He poured himself a drink, then headed to the bedroom to pack. The sound of his cell phone vibrating drew his attention away from the headstrong woman he'd forget if he could. Garth Garrison's name flashed across the screen. The man had been blowing up his phone all day. Alonso allowed the call to roll into voice mail.

Five minutes later, Alonso's phone rang again. This time Vivian's name populated the screen. An unexplainable excitement filled him. This call he would take.

He lifted the device. "Hello?"

A pause lingered as if Vivian contemplated whether or not to disconnect. Finally, her sweet voice danced over the line, melting away the hint of anxiousness that he'd felt just a moment earlier. This woman made him experience all types of unwelcomed emotions.

"Hi. Were you busy?"

If he had been, the answer would have still been, "No."

"So, I was thinking… If your invitation still stands, I'd like to tag along with you. If that's okay."

Alonso eased down onto his bed. "Are you sure that's a good idea?" The line grew so still he thought she'd hung up. A hint of alarm gripped him. "Hello?"

"I'm here."

Inwardly, he blew a sigh of relief. *Good.*

"It's for a good cause, so yeah, I'm sure. When are we leaving?"

He pumped his fist into the air. "Tomorrow morning at eight. But if that's too early…"

"Eight is fine. I guess I'll see you in the a.m."

"I look forward to it."

"Good night, Alonso."

A question lingered that he had to know the answer to. "Why did you change your mind?" It was a good cause when he was at her place.

"Because I have two hands. Good night."

The line went dead and Alonso pulled the phone away from his ear and stared at it. It would be a good night. But it was going to be an even better morning.

Chapter 9

From the minute they'd pulled out of her driveway, Alonso had kept Vivian entertained. For such a savvy business-man, he had a playful side she adored. After listening to his childhood tales, she was surprised the man still had all of his limbs. She couldn't remember the last time she'd laughed so hard.

Vivian couldn't believe she'd actually allowed Tressa to talk her into taking this trip with Alonso, but she was glad she had. And she really couldn't believe she hadn't jumped out of the Jeep Wrangler when he'd told her they'd be staying at a friend's beach house, instead of *separate* hotel rooms. She really, really couldn't believe how much she was looking forward to spending more time with him.

Alonso hadn't mentioned anything else about purchas-ing her house since their meeting at Caliente Mexicana. What was he waiting on? She knew this perfect gentle-man routine was all for show. She was sure the ball would drop soon and they'd return to their buyer-seller dynamic.

"Are you comfortable?" Alonso asked.

"Yes, thank you."

"Good. I'm glad you changed your mind. You'll like Infinity Island. There's no place like it on earth. Well, in my opinion. It's majestic."

Vivian laughed. "Really?"

Whatever lingered behind that wicked smile, he kept to himself. Admittedly, she thought the two-hour ride would be awkward. It'd been the complete opposite. "Your friend. How long has he lived on the island?"

Alonso chuckled, then tapped his thumb against the steering wheel. "About that... I have a confession."

Confession? Uh-oh. She knew things were going too well.

"It's not a friend's beach house. It's mine."

"Yours? You lied to me?" She wanted to be upset with him, but found even when she tried to be angry at him, she couldn't stay that way for long.

"No. I just omitted a few details."

"Lied. Why? Am I not worthy of your truth?"

Alonso's expression turned stern. Activating the turn signal, he pulled over onto a grassy knoll. Popping the gearshift into Park, he leaned toward her. "That's not it at all. I just thought if I told you it was my place you'd be reluctant to come. I didn't want you to think my motives were anything but sincere. This really is about volunteering. Nothing else."

The *nothing else* bothered her more than it should have, especially since it was the exact thing she'd told herself. That this trip was not about them. "Omitting details won't build trust." Alonso's brow arched in what she took as surprise.

"Is that what we're doing, building trust?"

"Everything is built on trust, even friendship. And what

better way to build trust than a road trip?" She smiled, tossing his words back at him.

Before Alonso could respond, her cell phone rang. Without even having to look at the screen she was sure it was Tressa calling to check on her.

"If I don't answer, Tressa will assume you chopped me up into tiny pieces and scattered my remains in the ocean."

"In that case, definitely answer it. I have a feeling I wouldn't want to get on Tressa's bad side."

"You're right. You don't."

Alonso veered back onto the road as she took the call. "Hi, Tress."

"Listen to you sounding all spunky. I was calling to check on you, but by the sound of your voice you're a-okay."

Vivian could feel Tressa smiling over the phone. "I am. We're about thirty minutes from the island."

"The island? That sounds so romantic. I'm so proud of you."

"Why?"

"Because you're finally getting back on the horse. And you've picked one hell of a stallion to mount."

Vivian cut a cautionary eye to Alonso. "Okay, I'm hanging up now."

"Wait, wait. Make sure you use protection. I am too young to be an auntie slash godmother. Just kidding. About the auntie-slash-godmother part. Not the protection part."

"Bye, Tressa."

"One more thing."

Vivian was afraid to ask. "What, silly woman?"

"I know you really like Alonso, but…if he doesn't go down on you, he's definitely not the one, sweetie. Love you. Have fun and many orgasms. Kisses."

The line went dead. Vivian pulled the phone from her ear and shook her head. Vivian could assure Tressa that this trip would not entail orgasms.

"Everything okay?"

"Yes. Just Tressa being Tressa."

"She seems like a good friend."

"She's the sister I never had. She's helped me through some trying times." Vivian refused to allow any thoughts of her ex to creep in and ruin her jovial mood. He didn't deserve any space in her head.

"Sounds like my best friend, Roth. The guy you briefly encountered in my office."

She recalled the handsome man.

"I would have introduced you, but seeing how you'd come for blood..."

"You are so dramatic. Just drive."

They shared a laugh. Alonso cracked his window and inhaled deeply.

"You smell that?"

Vivian drew in a deep breath. "I love the smell of the ocean."

"So do I."

Ten minutes later, they pulled up to a small security station. A wooden sign painted blue and white hung against the small building, Welcome to Infinity Island scrolled in fancy letters across the front. Alonso lowered the window and spoke to the young man there before proceeding forward.

Alonso had been right. Vivian fell in love with Infinity Island the moment they crossed the bridge. From the ranch-style, two-story and three-level homes in hues of coral, aqua, yellow and lavender to the grass so green it looked spray painted. And butterflies—they were everywhere—in vibrant hues, adding to the bursts of colors already present.

"So many butterflies," she said, more to herself than Alonso, absently fingering the butterfly charm on her bracelet. She thought about her father, a brief sadness washing over her.

"They're everywhere," he said. "Something about the island draws them."

Vivian understood that draw. Everything in Infinity Island seemed magnified. Even the sun appeared to shine brighter here. The air seemed crisper, the sky bluer. Could this place truly be magical? What she'd experienced the mere moments she'd been here opened her mind to the possibility.

Ha. What was she thinking? It only seemed mystical because it'd been a long time since she'd ventured somewhere so beautiful.

Alonso honked and waved at numerous people as they cruised down the unmarked road. Everyone seemed eager to see him, beaming smiles as they passed by. "Do you know all of these people?"

"Everyone knows everyone on the island."

Could be interesting. Maybe she'd learn some juicy tidbits about him. Vivian pointed to a large grass-covered lot. "What happens there?"

"Music on the Green every Saturday evening. Weather permitting. This weekend is Jazz Fest. We can go if you'd like."

"Sounds good."

After what felt like miles—and the end of the island—they arrived at a house that made Vivian's jaw drop. Unlike the other homes, this house had a personality all its own. The white-and-olive-colored three-level dwelling sat elevated off the shore. Vivian noted the stairs leading from the house down to the beach. This location—secluded from the rest of the island—and the house were both impressive. She wouldn't have expected anything less.

"I'll grab the bags if you want to take a look around."

"I'll help you first. Then I'll explore."

He nodded. "Cool."

The inside of the home was just as spectacular as the outside. State-of-the-art everything. The interior was decorated in neutral colors with dashes of beach blue here and there. Obviously seashells were the theme. There were seashell pictures, seashell art and actual seashells scattered about. "Did you decorate the place?"

Alonso chuckled. "No. If I had decorated, there would be a couple of lawn chairs and probably a tiki bar in the middle of the room. I hired out."

"Good idea."

"Hey. You got something against tiki bars?"

"Only ones adorning living rooms."

With his head, he directed her toward the stairs. "Come on. I'll show you to your floor."

Vivian's brow furrowed. "My...*floor*?"

"Yes. You have the entire second level to yourself. You'll have all the privacy you need. My bedroom is on the third."

Well, how could she argue with having her own floor? "Are there more bedrooms on the third floor, too?"

"No. Just mine."

"Your bedroom is the *entire* third floor?"

He chuckled again, and led her up the stairs. "I like space."

Apparently.

There were two humongous bedrooms on the second level, one outfitted in a crab theme, the other nets and starfishes. She chose the latter. Mainly for its panoramic window that gave her an unobstructed view of the ocean. Alonso pressed a button and the glass retracted into the wall. Yeah, she was going to like it here.

Outside her window, blue water stretched for miles, kissing the burned-orange horizon. There was no sound like that of the ocean making a mad dash toward the shoreline. Huge waves that dissolved into tiny ripples lapped at the creamy white sand below. Vivian inhaled a lungful of the crisp, salty ocean air, then closed her eyes and enjoyed the melody of gawking seabirds.

It'd been a long time since she'd felt this at peace. A gentle breeze caressed her skin, and a moan of contentment slipped past her lips.

"Do you need some privacy?"

Opening her eyes, she flashed a half smile. "Sorry."

"Don't be. It was a beautiful sound."

The heated look in his gaze made Vivian lose her train of thought. A warm sensation blossomed in her cheeks and traveled to the space between her legs. How could a simple look wreak so much havoc on her body?

Then it hit her.

There was nothing simple about his look. Primal. Confident. Hazardous, even. But nothing simple. The look he anchored to her was complex, daunting, foretelling. She yanked her attention away from him and placed it back on the ocean. "Can I ask you something, Alonso?"

"Sure."

"Why so much space? It seems like a lot for just one man."

Alonso folded his arms across his chest. The navy-colored fabric stretched under the strain of his bulging biceps. The image of being wrapped in his protective embrace danced in her head. *Stop it, Vivian. Just stop it.*

"Maybe one day it won't be enough."

Did that mean he wanted a family? A huge one if he intended to fill this place. There was something endearing about the declaration. Maybe because she wanted the same.

His hard stare burned a hole through her, but she didn't turn away. Couldn't turn away. Their connection tore through her like a raging beast vying for dominance. Powerful. Potent. Perilous.

They eyed one another for a long time, neither willing to take the loss that would result from turning away. But when his eyes lowered to her mouth, he gained an unfair advantage. A wave of fear crashed over her. The empowered woman she'd been mere seconds ago faded into a vulnerable damsel in distress who wanted to be saved. Needed to be saved. And only Alonso's kisses could do the trick.

But what if he did kiss her? What would she do? What *could* she? From prior experience, she knew that once his lips crushed down on hers, she'd be incapable of doing anything other than kiss him back.

This was hell. Hot. Damning. And the result of bad choices.

The phrase *home sweet home* played in her head. At home, she could escape. Here, where in the hell could she run?

"We should probably make a move to get lunch. After that, I'm sure you want to rest up and relax, as your vacation plans were to sleep. We have a big day tomorrow," Alonso said.

Maybe this wasn't hell, after all. The devil certainly would not have freed her so easily. In that heated, intense, all-consuming moment they'd shared, something became abundantly clear. She was fighting a battle. One she had little hope of winning.

But she would continue to fight the good fight for as long as she could.

Chapter 10

Alonso moved about the kitchen the following morning. Although he wasn't a fan of coffee, he could certainly use a big mug of it now. It'd been a restless night, because all night he'd dreamed about Vivian. Touching her, teasing her, kissing her, making love to her. At one point, he awakened so hard he thought his dick would snap off. Damn that woman for putting his mind, body and soul through such torture.

He'd chosen to remain a perfect gentleman and not kiss her in the bedroom the day before, but now he was kicking himself for not taking the opportunity to taste her mouth. Even if it'd only been for a few seconds. If it hadn't been for the look he saw flash in her brown eyes, maybe he would have.

Fear.

Was that what he'd seen in her eyes? If not fear, definitely uncertainty. Whatever it was had stopped him dead in his tracks. When Vivian came to him—and she would come to him *and* for him—he wanted her to do it willingly. Not from any kind of heat-of-the-moment action she would regret later.

"Morning."

Vivian's delicate voice struck him with a jolt of awareness. Damn, this woman did ridiculous things to his body. "Morning," he said, removing the breakfast casserole he'd prepared from the oven.

She slid onto one of the wood-and-leather barstools situated around the stone island. He wanted to ignore the way her hardened nipples pushed against the nightshirt she wore, but man, did they call to his lips. *"Shit."* He yanked his hand away from the hot dish he'd touched.

Alarm lit Vivian's face. She came off the stool and neared him. "Are you okay?"

Alonso shook his hand to remove the sting. "Yeah. Just a klutz. It's not serious. I'll just put some butter on it."

She led him to the sink. "Butter doesn't work for burns. That's an old wives' tale. In fact, it could do more damage. It could contain bacteria that could get into your wound."

Attractive and a wealth of knowledge.

"Plus, butter retains heat. You want to cool the burn down, which is why we need to run it under cool water for about five minutes. It will help soothe the pain."

Alonso's eyes raked over Vivian's features as she nursed him…again. If he hadn't known any better, he'd have thought he was subconsciously injuring himself just to get close to her. But then he remembered the paper cut hadn't been his fault.

Even with her hair pulled into a simple ponytail, she was gorgeous. Her skin was as smooth as silk. He noted the absence of makeup. She was a natural beauty.

Vivian's eyes rose to his. "How does it feel?"

"Better." The pain had actually dissolved. But he wasn't

convinced it was the cool water that had alleviated his discomfort; he was sure it'd been Vivian's gentle touch.

"Looks like just a first-degree burn. It's minor. You wouldn't happen to have any aloe vera gel, would you?"

"Sorry. Fresh out."

Vivian retrieved the first aid kit. After washing his index finger in soap and water, she wrapped it in sterile gauze. "You're really good at taking care of people." When she smiled up at him, he experienced a tightening in the pit of his stomach. Yeah, he had it bad for her.

"Thank you. You should be more careful when handling hot objects. You could have severely injured yourself."

Vivian ambled back to her seat. He was tempted to ask for instructions on how to handle her, because she was as hot as they came. By the cautious expression on her face, he was sure she had some idea of what was running through his mind.

Focus, Wright. Don't blow this. Alonso maneuvered with his good hand. "Well, after all of that, I hope you're still hungry."

"I'm not much of a breakfast eater, but it smells so good I don't know if I can resist you." Wide-eyed, she blurted, "It. I'm not sure I can resist *it*." Her eyes darted away from him to the glass dish. "Wh…" She cleared her throat. "What is it?"

He had a feeling she'd said exactly what she'd meant. She couldn't resist him. And that was exactly what he wanted. "An oven-baked spinach, cheese and sausage omelet. It also has tomatoes, garlic and onions in it."

"Yum. I'm in."

After a breakfast packed with laughter and endless chatter Alonso and Vivian dressed and headed out. It was amazing the difference thirty miles could make when dealing with a hurricane. Infinity Island had sustained a few displaced shutters and a downed tree limb here and there, but what Alonso was witnessing a bit farther up the coast was crazy.

Houses had been rocked off their foundations. Retreating waters had left roads littered with sand. High winds had claimed anything not nailed down. What appeared to have once been a deck was strewn in a water-logged yard. He adjusted his thoughts. The winds had apparently even claimed things that had been nailed down.

"This is crazy," he said absently.

"Yes, it is."

Alonso spotted a woman being consoled by someone he assumed to be her spouse. Judging by the carnage in the yard where they stood, they'd lost everything. His heart sank. He took a moment to count his blessings.

"These poor people," Vivian said, her tone shaky.

He imagined what this must have been doing to her. As hard-nosed as she pretended to be, he'd gotten a glimpse at a more fragile side of Vivian Moore. She cared. Dare he say, possibly cared too much? Carrying the weight of others' misery had to be exhausting.

"That's why we're here. To help them," he said.

She nodded, her eyes glassy. He willed her not to cry. If she did, he'd have no other choice but to veer to the side of the road and pull her into his arms. And if he pulled her into his arms, that would surely set off a chain reaction of reckless longing inside him.

Luckily, his fervent praying worked. Not a single tear slid down her cheek. A short time later, they pulled into a sand-spackled parking lot. DISASTER RELIEF was printed in large red letters on a sign attached to a brick building, visibly untouched by the hurricane.

Scoring one of the last available spaces, he killed the engine. The number of individuals filing into the volunteer check-in center surprised him. *A boost to humanity.* Humanity could definitely use all of the boosting it could get.

When Vivian reached for the handle, he stopped her. "I'll come around and help you out."

Protest danced in her eyes. If he had to guess, she'd been on the verge of telling him she was more than capable of exiting the vehicle without his assistance. But much to his surprise, the fight that had glowed on her face fizzled.

Apparently, she'd realized there were far more important things to focus her energy on. He hoped one of those things was him. Oh, the idea made him all warm and fuzzy inside.

Warm and fuzzy inside? He scolded himself. *Don't you ever say some shit like that again. You don't do warm and fuzzy. You do frigid and hard. You're a bull shark, not a damn guppy. Yeah.* The pep talk restored some of his manhood.

Moving to the passenger's side, Alonso opened the door, then offered his hand for Vivian to take. She didn't level any disapproving glances at him this time, which stunned him again. The second her hand was in his, a jolt of energy shot up his arm. What in the hell was this woman doing to his system?

"Watch your step. It's a bit slick in spots," he said.

Inside the building—a long abandoned veterans' hospital—an individual in a fluorescent green shirt marked STAFF directed them to where they needed to be. Since so many health professionals had answered the call for assistance, Vivian wasn't needed in a medical capacity. Instead, she'd been placed on debris retrieval, while he was on structural repair detail. It all sounded so official.

After sitting through a brief orientation, they were off.

Perched on a ladder, Alonso tried to focus on the gutter he'd been replacing. Unfortunately, his attention kept sliding to Vivian below. Every time she bent at the waist, his eyes did a happy dance. Damn, she wore those jeans well. *Focus, Wright.* That line was becoming his mantra.

He glanced at his wrapped finger. The last time he'd been caught up in Vivian's allure he'd damn near burned his whole finger off. Tumbling to his death would not be a good look. Refocusing on the gutter, he ignored the pull of the woman who was making him lose his damn mind.

The first thing Vivian did when they returned from their day of volunteer work was shower. Afterward, she'd joined Alonso on the deck, where he was grilling steaks and burgers they'd purchased on their way home.

Home? On the way to *Alonso's home*, she corrected.

And steaks *he'd* purchased. He hadn't allowed her to spend a dime. What was with him not wanting her to pay for anything? Then it hit her. She'd told him the story of her trifling ex running off with her money.

Maybe he was trying to show her he was not a deadbeat. No need. He'd long proved he was a far better man than her ex could ever hope to be. Alonso was thoughtful, compassionate, patient. Tyler was... Well, he was no Alonso, that was for sure.

Her eyes roved over his ass in the plaid shorts he wore, then burned a trail along his muscular legs and down to his big feet. She'd always heard big feet equal big meat. Nearly gnawing her lip off, she scolded herself for the roguish thoughts swimming through her head.

The polo shirt he wore accented his solid frame. Yellow was a good color on him. The only thing she disapproved of was the "Big Daddy on the Grill" apron he wore. Only because it covered a part of him she shamefully wanted a glimpse of. *Stop it, Vivian. Just stop it.*

Vivian hadn't realized how spent she was until her attempt to push herself from the red Adirondack chair she'd been lounging in. "Yow." She slinked back down.

Alonso eyed her over his shoulder. "What's wrong?"

She rolled her head on stiff shoulders. "I think I need a

deep tissue massage. All of the bending, twisting, kneeling and lifting has taken its toll."

Alonso placed the tongs down, wiped his hand on a towel and moved behind her chair.

Alarm set in when he hovered above her. "What are you doing?"

"Just sit back and enjoy the experience."

Before she could mount an effective protest, Alonso's big strong hands clamped down over her shoulders. *Pr-protest needed.* Instead, her body relaxed under his skillful kneading. *Okay. Another minute, then I'll protest. I'll definitely protest.* She closed her eyes and took pleasure in the attention Alonso was giving her. "*Mmm.* Harder." The yearning in her tone should have mortified her, but it'd been warranted. The man was good with his hands. Real good.

Alonso's tone was heavy and seductive when he said, "Your wish is my command."

He dug his fingers deeper into her weary muscles. Hadn't she just thought something about protesting? Was there truly a need to protest something as trivial as a shoulder massage?

Alonso's slow, thorough touch turned her skin into lava. Something urged her to glance up at him, and when she did, his intense stare took her breath away. Under the fire-packed scrutiny, she nearly burst into flames. How did he keep doing that to her? Why did she keep allowing it?

As if she had any other option.

Vivian wrinkled her nose, the smell of something pungent filling her nostrils. She snapped her head forward. Smoke billowed from the closed grill lid. "Fire!"

Alonso, clearly oblivious to the flames, continued to knead. "What?"

"*F-fire!*" This gave her the motivation she needed to get to her feet.

"*Shit.*" Alonso darted across the deck and lifted the lid.

Grabbing the long spatula, he shifted the charred meat out of contact with the flames. A couple minutes later, he had the fire extinguished.

He turned to her with a perplexed expression on his face. "Sooo, I was thinking… We should go out."

Not a bad idea. The less time they spent alone, the better.

Chapter 11

The mere sight of Vivian was becoming far more than Alonso could handle. And when she wore clothing like she had on now—a white fitted tank top and white-and-yellow skirt highlighting her gorgeous curves—it made being around her that much harder. In every sense of the word.

A warm breeze blew in off the water and her scent wafted toward him. *Cotton candy.* Whatever fragrance she wore made her smell like a carnival treat. Damn, he loved eating cotton candy. Maybe there'd be some in his near future. One could only hope.

But for now, he'd settle for having a low-key meal with her, since he'd turned their intended dinner into ash. Now that he thought about it, it wasn't solely his fault he'd nearly burned down his house. Vivian had to share some of the blame. If it wasn't for her sensual movement and her urging him to "do it harder," he would have never lost focus.

Actually, by his conclusion, she was more at fault than he was. Probably best to keep that to himself, though.

Alonso requested a table on the deck overlooking the water, at his favorite—and the only—restaurant on the island: Mama Tu's Seafood House.

"My boy," came from behind them.

Alonso would know that country drawl anywhere. *Mama Tu.*

Mama Tu moved toward him like an adoring fan to a celebrity. Once in reach, she swaddled him in her large arms. The embrace was affectionate, similar to a mother hugging her son. Or *how* a mother should hug her son. He really wouldn't know. He mimicked her enthusiasm, planting a kiss on the top of her salt-and-pepper hair, cornrowed in two thick braids.

Mama Tu cradled his face between her hands. "Oh, I'm so glad to see you. Now, let me look at you." She beamed as she scrutinized every inch of his face. "You're emitting some good energy. And you have a glow about you. Could this pretty thang have something to do with it?"

When Mama Tu set her attention on Vivian, Vivian's cheeks turned a rosy red. If there were really a glow on his face, Vivian had everything to do with it. He could sense Vivian's unease.

Alonso made the introductions. "Mama Tu, Vivian. Vivian, Mama Tu."

"Nice to meet you, Ms…Tu."

Alonso and Mama Tu both laughed.

"Everyone on this island calls me Mama Tu, and so will you. Now, come on over here and give Mama Tu a big ole hug."

When Mama Tu took Vivian into her arms, Alonso chuckled. Vivian seemed unprepared for the magnitude of the embrace. He understood. Mama Tu had a way of holding your soul captive—in a positive way. Vivian's eyes slowly closed and a look of calm appeared to wash over her.

Yeah, she was experiencing it. The phenomenon widely known on the island as the Mama Tu Effect.

Suddenly, Vivian's eyes popped open and she jerked away. "I'm sorry. I—"

Mama Tu sounded a hearty laugh. "Honey, folks have fallen asleep in my arms. My mother used to say I had the touch. That it guided people into the past, anchored them to the present and ushered them toward the future."

Mama Tu took Vivian's hand and led her across the wooden deck. Vivian tossed a glance over her shoulder, presumably to see if he was following. He wasn't letting her too far out of his sight. *That* she could count on.

"Best seat in the house," Mama Tu said.

Alonso had to agree. Though, in his opinion, there wasn't a bad spot located on the deck. Every table—whether the two-tops or the four-tops—had an excellent view of the ocean. The place was even more beautiful at night when the votive candles on the tables and tiki torches attached to the perimeter were lit. It was all so romantic.

Mama Tu wrapped an arm around Alonso's waist. "I'll leave you two alone. Remember, your money is no good here."

Alonso eyed the portly woman. "Do we have to have this argument every time?"

Mama Tu reached up and patted his cheek. "What am I going to do with you?"

Mama Tu strolled away before he could respond. He pulled out Vivian's chair, and she eased down. Below, an older couple walking hand in hand, smiling and laughing, caught his eye. That's what he wanted. A love that grew stronger with time.

"They're cute, huh?" Vivian said, following his stare.

He took a seat across from her. "Yes. The Jenkinses. They've been married since they were seventeen."

Vivian's brows arched. *"Seventeen?"*

He nodded. "They always say they're on a forty-plus-year honeymoon. You'll get to meet them at Music on the Green. Their energy is infectious."

"So would you say they emit good energy?" She smirked.

Had she just used Mama Tu's words against him? Good one. But he was sure he could do better. "Well, I would say it's a powerful energy. One that gets so *deep* inside of you that you feel it throughout your entire body. It starts off nice and slow, then morphs into something that takes complete control. You never want the sensational feeling to end. The more you want, the more it gives."

The amusement slid from Vivian's face and she swallowed hard. Yeah, he'd got her.

"That…um…sounds fascinating." She took an anxious sip from her water glass.

Alonso's eyes slid briefly to her lips. "It's a mind-blowing experience. You'll enjoy it. You have my word."

Vivian tangled her fingers together into a crazy web. If she continued, she would surely snap one. When she noticed his scrutiny, she slid her hands into her lap.

"Something to look forward to, I guess," she said.

Oh, he had a few things she could look forward to. When her tongue peeked out to wet her lips, he inwardly groaned. Damn, he wanted to taste her mouth again. Preferably while making sweet love to her.

Why had he promised himself he'd be nothing but a complete gentleman? Being gentlemanly was the last thing on his mind when he looked at Vivian. He'd also promised himself no business talk about her house. That promise he was sure he could keep, the former… Well, he'd just have to play it by ear.

Their waitress arrived at the most opportune time. Her intrusion allowed Alonso to clear his thoughts of tasting every inch of Vivian's magnificent body. He longed to hear

his name roll off her tongue. If he got his way, he would…
over and over again.

After giving their orders, they eyed each other again.

"Are you and Mama Tu related?"

"You could say that. She was one of the first people I
met when I bought the house here. From day one, she has
treated me like family."

"She reminds me so much of my grandmother."

Now he understood Vivian's reaction when Mama Tu
had pulled her into her arms. Vivian's gaze drifted away,
and she looked as if she was reliving a memory.

"I love this island," she said, snapping back to their
conversation.

"I knew you would."

Because of the flood of volunteers, Alonso and Vivian
had been told it wouldn't be necessary to report tomorrow, turning what had started as a humanitarian trip into
a weekend getaway.

Might as well take full advantage. "So, I was thinking…
Since we don't have to report for duty tomorrow, we should
head into Carolina Beach for a little retail therapy. There
are a ton of shops on the boardwalk you might like. What
do you think?"

"Um…sounds good."

Yes, it did, because it meant spending more time with
her.

The waitress returned a short time later with their orders. Four clusters of crab legs, steamed shrimp, french
fries and hush puppies for him; a seafood bake of shrimp,
crabmeat, sausage, potatoes and cheese for her.

Alonso mulled over her plate. "Are you going to share
your seafood bake? It's one of my favorites."

"No, my brother, you have to get your own."

He tossed his head back in laughter. "That's cold. I'd
share with you."

"I'll think about it."

When she brought the glass to her lips, he envied it. Was it possible to want anything more than he wanted Vivian? Something he wanted more than he wanted her... He couldn't think of one single thing.

Vivian watched Alonso check his caller ID again. The second time since they'd arrived at Mama Tu's. Apparently, someone wanted him. That seemed to be a theme, people wanting him. She refused to name herself as one of those people, even though she was.

"I'm sorry. I have to take this."

She nodded her understanding. Watching Alonso stroll away, she couldn't help wondering who was blowing up his line. Not that it was any of her business. Just curious. A discontented female trying to locate her man, perhaps?

No. She definitely wouldn't have been here if she thought Alonso was involved with someone. She might have been a whole lot of things, but a homewrecker was not one of them.

Why did it even matter who was calling? She and Alonso were just friends. No matter what the intense moments they'd shared all evening suggested. And even calling them *friends* might have been a stretch. *Social acquaintances.* Yeah, that sounded better.

"Mind if an old lady joins you?"

Vivian glanced up to see Mama Tu. "Please," she said, motioning for her to take a seat.

Mama Tu reminded Vivian so much of her grandmother it was scary. A presence that instantly drew you in, warm and welcoming, and knew how to throw down in the kitchen.

"I hope you enjoyed everything and saved room for my homemade banana pudding."

"It was the best meal I've had in months. As good as

banana pudding sounds, I don't think I can eat another thing." Vivian rubbed her stomach. "I'm stuffed."

"Well, I'll just have to pack you up some to go. I always like sending my boy away with something. Seeing how he never lets me comp his bill."

Vivian eyed the direction Alonso had walked. "Yeah, he seems to have a problem with people doing things for him."

"Men."

Vivian wanted to say *not all men*. Her ex had no problem allowing her to do it all.

"So, how long have you two been an item?"

An item? Her and Alonso? "No, we're not an item. We're just fr—" She stopped abruptly. "We're just social acquaintances." For some reason, the label made much more sense in her head.

"*Social acquaintances?* Hmm. Now, that's a new one. Well, you two give off a vibe like *intimate lovers*."

Yep, this was her grandmother reincarnated. Always said exactly what was on her mind. How in the heck was she supposed to respond to Mama Tu's declaration? Her cheeks burned with the awkwardness she felt. Luckily, someone summoned Mama Tu into the restaurant. Inwardly, Vivian blew a sigh of relief. Outwardly, she smiled dumbly.

"Lord, these folk can't go two minutes without yelling my name. It was a pleasure meeting you, Vivian. I got a feeling we'll be seeing each other plenty."

Mama Tu ambled off, taking a moment to chat with patrons—most she appeared to know by name. Well, Alonso had said everyone knew everyone on the island. And she figured if anyone knew anyone it was Mama Tu. The woman didn't strike Vivian as one who ever met a stranger.

I got a feeling we'll be seeing each other plenty. Did

Mama Tu mean before they left to head back home? *Of course*. What else could she have meant?

"I'll leave this here. No rush."

Vivian stopped their waitress from leaving. Retrieving the plastic black binder containing the bill, she placed enough inside to cover the check and provide a generous tip. The young girl thanked her and left.

Alonso finally returned to the table. "I'm sorry about that. Work."

Noting the perplexed expression on his face, she said, "Is everything okay?"

He sighed. "As good as it's going to get for now."

Whatever the call had been about had clearly stressed Alonso. It wasn't a look she was used to seeing on him. "Let's take a walk on the beach." She groaned to herself. Why had she just suggested something so cozy? But it wasn't like it was a late-night stroll under the moonlight. That would have been romantic. With the sun still high in the sky, this was innocent.

"Sure. Let me just take care of the bill." He motioned for their waitress.

"No need. I've already taken care of it." Alonso's brows furrowed as if he didn't quite comprehend what she'd said.

"You paid the bill?"

He actually appeared more troubled by the news than appreciative. This only-men-pay thing he had going on was becoming a bit archaic. "Yes, Alonso, I paid the bill. Is there a problem?"

His luscious lips parted but closed a second later. Obviously he thought twice about whatever he was about to say. Smart move. She would hate to have to put him in his place in front of all these people. She didn't understand the big deal. Men and their egos.

Alonso tossed out an unenthusiastic "Thank you."

"You're welcome."

He stood, then moved to her chair to assist her up. If nothing else, he certainly was a gentleman. After informing Mama Tu they would be back later for their to-go goodies, they made their way down to the beach.

Vivian held her strappy sandals in her hand as they strolled. She liked the feel of the sand between her toes. It'd been a long time since she'd visited the coast. Far too long, she now knew.

Alonso hadn't said much since they'd left the restaurant. She wasn't sure if it was the phone call or the fact she'd paid the bill that had him withdrawn.

"Can I ask you something, Alonso?"

He nodded.

"Why does it bother you so much that I paid for dinner?"

Something fueled this behavior. He had to know she'd eventually ask. When he didn't readily answer, she assumed he was toying with the idea of baring his soul.

"There was a girl I really liked. I was eighteen, nineteen. I finally convinced her to go out on a date with me. I wanted to impress her, so I took her to this swanky Italian restaurant. I wasn't doing all that well back then financially, but I'd saved what I'd thought I needed to show her a good time."

"Confidence is preparation. Everything else is beyond your control." When she saw the quizzical expression on his face, she added, "It's something my grandmother used to say."

"Your grandmother was right, because my confidence was the only thing that went as planned. And by the end of the date, even that was crushed."

Now Vivian was really interested. "What happened?"

"I never anticipated this hundred-pound ballerina would eat as much as a Clydesdale horse."

Vivian burst into laughter. "A Clydesdale?"

"Yeah. I don't know where she packed it all. It was like she had a second stomach."

This brought more laughter from them both.

"It was actually impressive. Anyway, when the waiter brought the check, it exceeded what I had in my wallet. She wound up paying. Talk about a blow to a brother's ego."

When Alonso's expression went from jovial to somber, Vivian had a feeling the story would get worse.

He stared straight ahead. "I'll never forget the look of disgust I saw in her eyes that night. Like she'd come to the conclusion I was beneath her."

Vivian stopped and looked at him with tender eyes. Now she understood. But did he fear she would look at him the same way? Did he believe she was that petty? "If only she could see you now."

"I stopped needing to prove myself to people a long time ago."

Vivian wasn't wholly convinced that was true. Wasn't that part of the reason why he was there with her? To *prove* he could convince her to sell her childhood home to him? Whether he admitted it or not, he had an agenda. Most men did. Alonso was an excellent businessman. He wouldn't forfeit an attempt to try to sway her. It was just a matter of time. But for now, she would continue to play his game.

They started to walk again.

Vivian wrapped herself in her arms. "I think Infinity Island gets more and more beautiful by the second."

"Yes, it does."

The way Alonso spoke the words drew her attention. His gaze was bolted to her, and she got the impression they were talking about two totally different things. "Can we sit for a while?"

"Sure. I wish I had a blanket or towel for you to sit on."

"Sitting in the sand doesn't bother me." But she appreciated his thoughtfulness.

They'd sat and chatted so long, the sun had started to make its descent below the horizon. Orange, yellow and blue painted the sky in passionate hues. Under the right conditions, this could be considered ultraromantic. But not these conditions. They were just two fr— Social acquaint— *People* enjoying a sunset in what she was convinced was the most majestic place on earth.

A cool breeze blew in from the ocean. Vivian closed her eyes and allowed her head to recline back. She imagined Alonso pressing his lips to the hollow of her throat, dragging his tongue to her mouth and kissing her until they both neared loss of consciousness. Her lips curled at the fantasy.

"Why are you smiling?"

He'd been watching her. Meeting his gaze, she said, "I was thinking I could get used to beach living."

"Well, you can use my house anytime you'd like. Just let me know in advance."

"In case you have a romantic rendezvous planned?" She regretted the words the second they'd slipped out.

"You never know."

She turned away from him before her eyes revealed how much the idea of him rendezvousing bothered her. What was happening to her? Why did Alonso have her so twisted? She wasn't looking to be wooed. Wasn't looking for a relationship. And definitely wasn't looking for love. So what in the hell was the problem?

Sex? Could that be the issue? Did her drought have her hallucinating, feeling things that just weren't there? Like the catapult-you-to-the-moon chemistry between her and Alonso. Was it all in her head?

Maybe she should sleep with him as Tressa had suggested. Then she'd be cured.

Alonso, let's screw.

Ha!

As if she'd ever have the nerve to be so bold. Plus, everything was going so smoothly. Why upset the balance with sex? Pointless sex at that. Wait. Pointless? No, she was sure a roll in the sheets with Alonso would hold plenty of purpose.

Silence fell between them again as they set their gazes on the splendor of the Atlantic. She actually enjoyed being there with Alonso. Did he feel the same way about being there with her? No. For him, this was strictly business—masked in a humanitarian effort that no longer existed.

Why were they still on the island? Shouldn't they have headed back to Raleigh after learning they were no longer needed? He hadn't made the suggestion and neither had she.

"I'm glad you came, Vivian," Alonso said, never pulling his eyes away from the water. "I've enjoyed hanging out with you."

She slid her attention to him, and when he gave her his in return, something sparkled in his eyes. *Just business*, she reminded herself.

Chapter 12

Vivian browsed inside a trinket shop while she waited for Alonso to finish up a call. The Carolina Beach shop was a hoarder's dream. You name it, it was available there. Including a neon pink dildo the size of a nuclear missile. She lifted the box to read the description.

"Jesus," she mumbled to herself, examining the over-size toy. "Who in the hell would use this?"

"You'd be surprised."

Vivian jumped at the masculine voice behind her. As if coordinated with his arrival, the mammoth-size sex toy fell out the bottom of the box and landed on the floor by her feet. Urgently, she shifted to face the stranger.

His skin was smooth and creamy and the color of almond butter. Long black wavy hair was pulled back into a ponytail. Shirtless, his entire left arm was tattooed. Her eyes slid to what looked like a shark's tooth hung from a string around his neck. He was handsome, but not in a commanding, hold-your-eyes-hostage kind of way. In other words, he wasn't Alonso.

Her cheeks warmed as he scrutinized her and the empty box in her hand. "I was…um…" She laughed. "There's absolutely nothing I can say that'll undo this, is there?"

"No. But that's okay. If it's any consolation, a lot of women have the same reaction to the Pink Pounder. It's one of my best sellers."

"As only a gag gift, I hope."

"You never know." His cinnamon-colored eyes narrowed on her. "I haven't seen you around here before. Which means you must be a tourist."

"Guilty."

A smile curled his lips. "Maybe I can—"

"There you are."

Alonso's smooth tone massaged over her skin. He neared them with nothing but confidence in his step. Even fully clothed, he did hellacious things to her libido.

Alonso studied the box in her hand, then lowered his eyes to the dildo at her feet. A slow smile curled his lips. "She'll take it."

Vivian gasped. "What? No, I won't."

Alonso fished his wallet from his back pocket. "You have to get a souvenir, right? How much, my man?"

Vivian pulled at the hem of Alonso's shirt as he neared the cash register. "Alonso, if you buy that abomination, I'm going to bop you over the head with it."

"I'm not sure you can actually lift it that high. Either way, I'll take my chances."

She attempted to keep Alonso from passing the dildo peddler the money.

"You two are one of the funniest couples I've ever had in my shop."

This stilled Vivian. *Couple?* Why did he think they

were a couple? Probably because Alonso was trying to purchase her a big, plastic dick.

Neither she nor Alonso corrected him. Surrendering, she allowed Alonso to complete the transaction. As they exited the shop, Alonso offered her the bag containing the *souvenir* he'd purchased her. "You purchased it. You carry it."

"I'm not ashamed to carry an enormous penis around town. I've been doing it for years." A second later, he groaned and bit down on his bottom lip. "I apologize. For a second, I thought you were one of the guys."

She took that as a compliment. "You should be sorry. Especially for exaggerating like that." Yeah, she knew how to roll with the punches.

He barked a laugh. "All right. I walked right into that one."

They moved farther along the boardwalk, scoping out the eclectic array of shops along their route. So far she'd purchased a ceramic turtle, a wreath fashioned out of seashells and a stuffed dolphin. Actually, she hadn't purchased anything. Each time she'd tried to pay, Alonso would thwart her attempt. She didn't necessarily like it, but he left her little recourse.

"Come on in here, suga. I see you looking."

Vivian and Alonso looked at each other, then the petite woman urging them into Blanche's Lingerie Shop. Vivian had been eyeing the spot, but there was no way she'd enter with Alonso on her heels.

Alonso took her by the elbow. "We shouldn't be rude," he whispered, then led her in before she could protest.

Once inside, Vivian greeted the two older women browsing. Clearly, sexy had no age limit.

The woman who'd urged them inside set her sights on Alonso. "Suga, you look like a man who loves to see his woman in lingerie."

Alonso massaged his beard. "I'm not against it."

"Good. I'm Blanche, by the way. I own this little slice of heaven."

Blanche stood around five foot three, had brownish-blond hair and flawless makeup. Several tattoos covered her arms: a whip, chains, handcuffs and a red stiletto boot. She wore black leather shorts and a blue tube top. If Vivian had to guess, she would say Blanche was somewhere in her late fifties.

"I'm Alonso and this is Vivian."

Blanche threaded her arm through Alonso's. "You two make a stunning couple. And I'm not just saying that to get you to buy something."

Again with the couple thing. What kind of vibe were they giving off? "We're not a coup—"

"You're the second person to say something similar, Ms. Blanche. Thank you."

Vivian's mouth gaped but nothing came out. Had he just let Ms. Blanche believe they were a couple?

"Drop the *Ms.*, suga. I'm not that old." Blanche eyed Vivian. "Hun, why don't you take a look around. I'm gonna steal your fella for a moment. I've got something I think he'll like. It just came in yesterday."

He was not her fella. But instead of stating that, Vivian nodded. Alonso flashed an innocent expression, then shrugged as Blanche led him away. Vivian scowled at him. Oh, he was eating this up.

"What size is she?" Vivian heard Blanche ask.

"A twelve," Alonso said without hesitation.

How did he— *Details.*

Well, since she was here, might as well take a quick look around before Alonso and Blanche returned. Vivian browsed the collections of sensual wear that ranged from tame to why wear anything at all. There were a few sexy pieces that caught her eye. But who in the hell would she wear it for?

"Whoa! Sweet baby Jesus. *Yes!*"

Vivian jerked toward the direction of Alonso's voice. What in the hell had Blanche shown him? Her cheeks warmed when the two women glanced at her and snickered. A nervous smile curled her lips, her face burning from embarrassment.

What kind of outlandish getup had Blanche shown Alonso to warrant such a reaction? On second thought... didn't matter. It was no concern of hers. She returned her attention to the rack. How impressive could the lingerie have been anyway?

"I don't think she's adventurous enough to wear that, Blanche."

Vivian shot a narrow-eyed gaze in Alonso and Blanche's direction again. "Not adventurous enough," she whispered to herself. *How would he know how adventurous I am? Oh, I can show him adventurous. I'm plenty adventurous.*

Then it hit her. Did she come off as a prude? Vivian dismissed the idea. *Doesn't matter. Doesn't matter at all.* She didn't have anything to prove to Alonso Wright. And for the record, he couldn't handle her in lingerie.

When Alonso resurfaced from the back, he had his cell phone pressed against his ear. "I'll be right back," he mouthed.

Not that damn phone again. She nodded and watched him stroll through the exit. The way he ran his hand over his head reminded her of the first time she'd seen him at the hospital. He looked just as hassled now as he had then. She guessed any woman who fell for Alonso would have to put up with him being a workaholic. Luckily, neither appealed to her—falling for him nor his workaholic personality.

Tempted to request to see what had gotten Alonso so

excited, she resisted. She didn't need one more thing clouding her brain. Alonso had that part of the market cornered. Done with her lingerie experience, Vivian said goodbye to Blanche—who gave her a business card and welcomed her back anytime—and ambled outside.

Alonso's raised tone instantly snagged her attention. She eased toward the sound of his voice, then reconsidered. But something caught her ear.

"The house is as good as mine, but there's a ch—"

A knot formed in the pit of Vivian's stomach. *The house is as good as mine.* Was he referring to *her* house? The rope tightened. Of course he was. His claim infuriated her. But hadn't she been expecting this?

On the beach the day before, she'd actually considered that maybe—just maybe—this trip wasn't all about Alonso trying to get what he wanted. He'd proved her wrong. He was a businessman before all else.

She hurried away when it sounded as if he was finishing up the call. A mix of rage and something else she couldn't quite label swirled inside her.

The house is as good as yours, huh? Well, we'll just see about that.

Chapter 13

Vivian had been quiet for most of the drive back from Carolina Beach. And she'd been just as reserved once they'd arrived back at the house. Even now, as she helped Alonso plate dinner, she was in her own world. What she'd heard played over and over in her head, but instead of confronting him, she'd chosen to wait. Timing was everything.

When Alonso bumped her playfully, she jerked away. She'd be the first to admit she wasn't doing a good job at hiding her displeasure with him. But didn't she have a right to be angry as hell?

"Okay. What's going on, Vivian? I've tried my damnedest to figure out what I've done to piss you off, but nothing pops out at me."

Her first instinct was to tear into him for making her actually believe he could be about something more than business, but in good conscience, she couldn't. As much as she wanted to blame him, it wasn't his fault that she'd seen something that just wasn't there. It wasn't his fault that she'd allowed herself to actually believe they'd shared a connection.

"Nothing," she said, mounting a footstool to reach a dish on the top shelf. Despite her best efforts to wrangle her resentment, it grew. At this point, she wasn't sure if she were more furious at Alonso or herself. Alonso, for being a deceitful bastard. Herself, for being blinded by his illusion.

Not following her gut instinct had gotten her in one fine mess.

"Pardon my French, but I'm calling bullshit, Vivian."

She whipped around to face him, momentarily forgetting her present standing. The bowl flew from her hand as she fought to maintain her balance. The ceramic dish made a loud *ting* as it bounced off the counter and hit the floor, shattering into several large pieces.

Mentally bracing herself for the violent introduction she was about to make with the tiled floor, she closed her eyes and prepared for impact. Only it wasn't hard and cold that greeted her; it was firm and warm. When she cracked one eye open, Alonso's face was the first thing she saw.

"I got you," he said.

His sexy lips curled into a half smile that sent a wave of ravenous desire through her. Obviously her body hadn't gotten the memo from her brain that they were standing united *against* this man, not for him. But before she could even fully process the command to escape from his embrace, his mouth crashed down on hers and he kissed her with the fervor and intensity of a well-acquainted lover.

Alonso's tongue swept her mouth with a force she couldn't recall ever experiencing in all of her years of kissing. Instinctively…or voluntarily…or involuntarily…or desperately…however you wanted to label it, she matched his zeal. His arms tightened around her, pinning her even closer to his solid chest. Her heart pounded with so much force, she was sure he felt it. But she felt something, too. His hardness, pressing against her stomach.

Vivian wanted to pull away. God knew, she wanted to pull away and free herself from the consequences that could result from his kisses, her desire, their unrestrained chemistry. Chemistry that she'd attempted to dispel only moments earlier. But she couldn't pull away. Despite her best effort to convince herself this was nothing more than another trap Alonso was laying for her, she couldn't break free.

As if the god of coherent thinking felt sorry for her, it intervened, reminding her of the phone call she'd overheard earlier. The one all but assuring whomever Alonso had been talking to that the house—*her* house—was as good as his.

With fury overshadowing longing, she tore away from his delicious mouth and shoved out of his arms. "Was this your plan all along? Seduce me until I signed on the dotted line? Then discard me like you have every other woman in your life? Well, I have news for you, *Mr. Wright*, I'm not that damn easy. I'm leaving." She turned to escape the room.

"If that is what you think that kiss was about, you're deluding yourself, Vivian. You and I both know it was about far more. You can deny it now, but you can't deny it forever. It's too powerful."

The confidence in his tone, the control he exhibited, it all infuriated her even more. She stopped dead in her tracks, considering whether to turn and confront the foolishness he'd just spewed or simply keep walking. Unfortunately, he didn't give her the opportunity to react.

He neared her as he spoke. "You don't see me, Vivian. Not the man I truly am. You see all the men who have lied to you, deceived you. Your ex, your exes, maybe even your father."

With the mention of her father—a damn good man—she whirled around to face him. "Don't you ever talk about my father," she said, her voice shaky with emotion. His nearness unnerved her. And when she took a step back, she bumped into the island. Alonso braced a hand on either side of the island, pinning her in place.

A beat of silence played between them. Any other time, the way his commanding eyes probed her would have caused an instant stirring in her stomach. Not this time.

"What are you afraid of, Vivian? Are you afraid that if you look close enough, you might just like what you see?"

"I heard your phone call earlier. The one where you all but assured whomever was on the other end that my house is yours." She witnessed a subtle shift in Alonso's demeanor. Yeah, she'd doused some of his self-assurance. "Based on that, who should I be seeing?"

Without missing a beat, he said, "You should see the man who's fantasized about kissing you from the first time he ever laid eyes on you."

She wasn't swayed by his dime-store poetry.

"Or the man who hasn't been able to stop thinking about you since that day in the hospital."

Yeah, she was sure he'd thought about her. But only how he would bamboozle her.

"Or the man who loses his cool around you because he doesn't want to say something stupid and scare you off."

When she turned her head away, he placed a finger under her chin and directed her attention back to him.

"Or the man who can conduct business with some of the most powerful individuals in the country, without flinching, but can't keep his thoughts straight when you're around. See that man, Vivian. He's the only one who counts."

Vivian released a condescending laugh. "This is all a game to you, isn't it? You'll do or say whatever it takes to get what you want, not caring who you hurt in the process. And I was foolish enough to believe…" Her words trailed off. "I understand why you're so successful."

"You are absolutely right."

At least he was man enough to admit it.

"But only about the house. I wanted your house. I never made that a secret. *Wanted.* Past tense. Not anymore. There's something I want much more. Something I believe is exceedingly more valuable. You. I want you."

Vivian's breath seized in her chest from the sheer sincerity she witnessed in Alonso's eyes. Swallowing hard, she did her best to retain some semblance of control.

"You're afraid," he continued. "You're afraid of this thing we have going on." He cradled her face between his hands. "This wild, insane, all-consuming energy we generate. You don't trust it. You don't trust *it* because you don't trust *me*. But that's okay. You will."

"Always the businessman. Say what you need to, to get what you want."

"I want you. I want you," he repeated as if she hadn't heard him the first two times. "I've never wanted anything or anyone more. Tell me you don't want me, too."

"I don't—"

"*Liar.* You want me just as much as I want you."

His hands slid to her neck and he pulled her mouth closer to his, but instead of kissing her—something she shamelessly craved—he spoke in a gentle tone against her lips.

"You want me. You want me to kiss you until you're inches from unconsciousness."

"I don't." Though the longing in her tone would have suggested otherwise.

"You want me to strip every piece of clothing off you and caress your beautiful body."

"I don't." Her tingling flesh screamed the opposite.

"You want me to tease your nipples with my fingers, then my mouth."

"No... *I don't.*" However, her beaded nipples supported his claim more than her own.

"You want me to drag my tongue down the center of your torso, plant my face between your thighs and claim every drop of your wetness. Afterward, you can call Tressa and tell her that I might just be the one."

Vivian gasped and her eyes popped open. Had he heard Tressa over the phone? Clearly he had.

As if he hadn't tortured her enough, he continued with his arousing wordplay, "I want to taste you until you shiver. Until you beg me to enter you. And I will. Slowly and gently at first."

Until she begged? In his dreams. She didn't beg for anything.

Vivian swallowed hard again, her breathing so ragged from the impact of Alonso's assertions that she became dizzy. When she attempted to speak, her voice hitched. Clearing her throat, she started again. "I—I don't want any of that. Now, please...get out of my way."

The clammy, trembling hands she rested against his chest had been meant to push him away; instead, they explored his rock-hard frame. Once she realized what she'd been doing, she jerked away, her eyes wide in mortification, panic, dismay. "Oh, God, I... I..."

"'Want you, Alonso.' Say it, Vivian."

Her mind said no, but her body said, "I..."

"'Want you to make me climb the wall, Alonso.' Just say it, and I'll give you exactly what you want. Over and over again."

Vivian's heart wasn't the only thing thudding hard enough to rattle her bones. If the space between her legs could emit sound, it would be the piercing wail of a nuclear reactor warning of a potential meltdown. She neared critical status.

"Say it, Vivian. Say it so I can put us both out of our misery."

"I…want… I want you, Alonso." The choppy words were out before she even realized they were coming.

Alonso's mouth was on her before she'd even released the last syllable. He kissed her. Really kissed her. Made mad, raw, passionate love to her mouth. And she wanted it. Every inch, every stroke of his delicious tongue.

When he broke away, they both panted like heat-exhausted puppies needing water. But it wasn't water they needed—or wanted.

Without warning, Alonso scooped her into his arms and hurried for the stairs. Inside his bedroom, he placed her feet on the floor, but guided her body against one of the walls.

"Alonso, I want—"

"Shh." He pecked her gently. "I know what you want, remember?"

By the gleam in his eye, she knew he did.

He grabbed the hem of her shirt and lifted it over her head, dropping it to the floor where it formed a puddle at their feet. He kneaded her nipples through the blue fabric of her bra. A soft moan escaped past her lips. *"Mmm."* Removing the lacy material, he replaced his fingers with his warm lips. The sensation shot volts of pleasure through her entire body. "I want you right now. Please."

When Alonso returned to a full stand, he smirked. "I told you I'd have you begging."

"Don't let it swell your head."

"Much too late."

His eyes lowered to the tented front of his shorts and hers followed. The sight only amplified her anticipation.

Alonso captured her hand and guided it onto his erection. "See what you did."

She gripped him, explored him, stroked him gently. "Oops."

Taking both her hands into his, he pinned them against the wall above her head and ground his hardness against her. "It's going to be a long night."

"Show-off."

"You ain't seen nothing yet." He winked, then lowered to his knees.

Removing her skirt and panties, he kissed along her outer thigh, then the inner. Her eyes fluttered closed at the feel of him placing kisses against the curly hairs covering her core.

When Alonso placed one of her legs over his shoulder, then the other, her eyes sprang open. "What are—" She gasped when he slowly stood and her body glided up the wall. "Alonso—"

"Trust me enough to know that I got you."

When he'd mentioned making her climb the wall, she'd had something totally different in mind. She never imagined he literally meant she'd climb an actual wall. It was a good thing she wasn't afraid of heights, because her current position would have caused a full-on panic attack. Thank goodness for the high ceilings.

Vivian mounted a protest in her head...until Alonso's tongue found its way inside her, halting any objections she had. *"Oh, God."* His hands gripped her ass, while hers held his head in place. If she plummeted to her death at that moment, she'd go a very happy woman.

Several explicit words—that would have made a sailor blush—swam through her head. And when Alonso performed some impressive tongue action, she cried out so loud it vibrated her chest.

Her stomach muscles tightened, toes curled and breathing grew choppy as the powerful orgasm gripped her. Despite her squirming, Alonso held her firmly in place as he continued to feast on her. And just when she thought her body had no more to give, another even more potent orgasm claimed her. She wasn't sure how Alonso had managed to keep her upright, but he did.

This second release rendered her useless. Alonso cradled her spent body in his arms and carried her to the bed. Placing her down like a priceless artifact, he stood over her, his eyes raking over her nude frame as if trying to burn the image of her into his memory.

"You're so damn beautiful," he said.

"I want to see your body naked."

"Then you should tell me to take off my clothes."

"Take off your clothes," she said.

He smirked, then peeled the T-shirt from his body. The urge to reach out and glide her fingertips over his chocolate flesh rushed her, but she resisted. "Keep going."

Alonso unfastened his shorts and slowly lowered the zipper. Vivian held her breath as he hooked his thumbs inside his shorts and lowered them. Gnawing at her bottom lip, her excitement grew.

The gray fitted boxer briefs rode low, revealing his tantalizing V. Her eyes trailed the line of fine black hairs to the massive bulge that threatened to snake out the bottom of the underwear. Again, Alonso hooked his thumbs inside and inched the fabric down. His erection sprang free and bobbed in her direction.

Retrieving his wallet from the nightstand, Alonso fished out a gold wrapper, ripped into it and started to sheath himself.

"Let me," Vivian said.

Alonso arched a brow, then removed his hand. She held his eyes as she slowly rolled the latex down the length of him. He was so warm, so solid, so delicate to the touch that she wanted to toss the condom aside and take him into her mouth.

She didn't.

The selfish need to feel him inside of her held precedence. The second she was done, Alonso had her on her back, his body blanketing hers. When he inched inside of her—slow and gentle, like he'd promised—she moaned.

His soft lips pressed a kiss to her throat. "I love that sound."

Her eager hands glided along the length of his body as he delivered unhurried strokes. This felt good. He felt good.

"Is this what you wanted?" he asked, brushing a kiss against her jawline.

"Yes."

"I'm going to take my time with you, Vivian. Is that okay?"

"Yes." He repositioned her leg and she swore she felt him go even deeper.

"You taste great, but you feel even better." He kissed a corner of her mouth. "We're not going to get much sleep tonight, because I plan to be inside of you all night long."

She had no objections to that.

Alonso captured her mouth in a heady kiss. His strokes grew faster, harder with each brush of her tongue against his. She welcomed each powerful thrust delivered. Before long, he had her body in a frenzy and teetering dangerously close to the edge.

When she couldn't hold back any longer, Vivian broke her mouth away and cried out from the fire coursing through her. "Alonso... Alonso..." Her nails dragged across his damp flesh. "Don't stop."

His tempo grew clumsy and his breathing ragged. A sound that was a mix between a growl and a groan rumbled in his chest. *"Shit."* Several lumbering strokes later, he exploded.

The feel of him throbbing inside of her energized her body again, sending more ripples of pleasure through her. Moments later, Alonso collapsed next to her, cradling her against his warm, moist chest.

In a heavy breath, he said, "That was amazing."

She had to agree.

"There was one thing missing, though."

Vivian lifted her head to eye him. "What?"

"We didn't get to utilize your new toy."

She swatted him playfully. "No way are you coming near me with that abomination."

After a humorous moment, things settled.

Vivian placed her head back on Alonso's chest, the sound of his heartbeat drumming in her ear. "Just so we're clear, this doesn't change anything. I'm still not selling you my house." Her words were more good-natured than patronizing. She kissed the space under his chin just to make sure he knew that.

Alonso released a hearty laugh. "I have all that I want." He kissed her forehead and pulled her a little more snugly against him, held her a little tighter.

This doesn't change anything? Who in the hell was she kidding? This changed everything.

Chapter 14

When Alonso collapsed onto the bed, belly down, Vivian lay on top of him. The feel of her warm, naked body aroused him. What in the hell was she doing to him? They'd made love on and off for the past several hours, and he still couldn't get enough of her.

Vivian kissed his shoulder and fine bumps prickled his skin. Yeah, there was something special about this woman. He'd suspected it, but now knew for sure. "Are you hungry?"

They'd slept, chatted and ate in between their love-making sessions. He needed to stay nourished to keep up with Vivian. A rabbit didn't have anything on her. And as good as she felt to him, he planned to make love to her as much as she—and his body—would allow.

She nibbled on him. "Not for food."

"Damn, woman, I thought I was insatiable. You're wearing a brother out."

"It's been a while. Apparently, my body is trying to replenish itself."

"Well, I don't mind supplying the necessary sustenance you need."

"And you supply it so well."

"Careful. You're going to swell my head."

"Promises, promises."

"Wow. I never took you for a nympho."

Vivian playfully pinched him. "I'm not a nymphomaniac. I just enjoy having sex with you."

"I enjoy having sex with you, too." When he reached back and pinched her butt, she squealed. Her laughter made him smile. He liked the idea of being the one responsible for the jovial sound.

Vivian sobered, then rested her head flat against him. "Can I ask you something, Alonso?"

"No, you can't borrow any money."

"I'm serious," she said, thumping his ear.

Alonso's thoughts briefly moved to a memory of his mother. She used to thump him the same way when he was being a clown—which had been quite frequently. *The good times.* Those were the memories of his mother he liked to recall. Those were the ones he held dear to his heart.

Returning to present time, he said, "Sure."

"When were you stabbed?"

His body impulsively stiffened. He'd expected the question eventually. The night he'd stood shirtless in her laundry room, he'd spied her examining his wound. She hadn't inquired then, but he knew it was only a matter of time.

"Several years ago. When I first started out, I couldn't afford a posh downtown location. The place I could afford wasn't in the most luxurious part of town. One night I worked much later than I usually did. It was about one or two in the morning when I left the office."

"One or two in the morning?"

"That was customary. I was determined to succeed. I had to succeed. That meant sacrifice. Late nights, no days off, no social life, no sleep."

"No relationship."

"That, too."

"So you left the office…"

"I'd ordered Chinese and didn't want to leave the containers in the trash can overnight and stink up the place, so I carried them out with me. The Dumpster was located in the alley next to the building."

Vivian's head rose. "Uh-oh."

Obviously Vivian had a good idea of where this story was headed. He took a deep breath and continued. "Three young dudes popped out of nowhere. When they tried to rob me, I fought back."

"Alonso!"

"I know, I know. But I was young, dumb, hotheaded and cocky back then. I couldn't let these jokers punk me." He laughed. "They were whupping my ass good, but I managed to get in a few good shots." He sobered. "Then one of them pulled a knife."

Vivian gasped as if she'd been watching it all unfold right before her eyes.

"Next thing I know, I'm reeling on the cold, damp ground in excruciating pain. Barely conscious, I hear all of this commotion—cracking, groans, wails. A body fell next to mine, wrenching in obvious pain. I realized it was one of the thugs who'd attacked me."

Excited, she said, "The police had arrived."

"No. Hamilton."

"Hamilton?"

He chuckled at the surprise in her tone. "Yes, Hamilton. He stepped on the scene like the bionic man, tossing those cats like confetti. Long story short, Hamilton saved my life. I've been looking out for him ever since."

"So that's the connection between the two of you. I knew it had to be something that ran deep. You two have an amazing bond."

Alonso blew a heavy breath. "Wow. I just keep telling you sad shit from my past. I don't like talking about sad shit from my past with anyone. Including Roth and Hamilton." When Vivian kissed his ear, he shivered. That was his spot.

"You know why you keep telling me things?"

"Enlighten me."

"Because deep down you know you can trust me with it."

Alonso maneuvered until he was on his back and Vivian was resting on his chest. He studied her a moment. "Can I really?"

"Yes."

"I trusted a woman once. It didn't turn out so well."

"That just means you trusted the wrong woman. You can trust me with anything you want to share. I'll never judge you."

When she traced his lips with her index finger, he sucked it into his mouth.

"Tell me," she said.

Alonso's brow furrowed. "Tell you what?"

"How your ex betrayed you."

He ran his hand over his beard. Why did she keep forcing him to purge? "We'd been together about eight months or so. I was finally starting to make a name for myself. She—Inez—kept hinting toward marriage, but I wasn't ready to take that step. I couldn't provide like I needed to."

"Did you love her?"

"I thought I did."

"What ended the relationship?"

"She stopped taking her birth control pills because she said they were making her sick. I started wearing condoms again. I wasn't ready to be a husband, so I damn sure wasn't prepared to be a father." He blew a heavy breath. "I discovered she'd been poking holes in the condoms."

"Wow."

"I guess she figured if she got pregnant, I would have to marry her."

"Would you have?"

"Yes. I know what it's like growing up without a father."

A hint of sympathy flashed in Vivian's eyes. He wasn't sure which situation she pitied more—the shady ex or the absent father. They were equally troubling. But he'd gotten over both. He lifted his head and kissed the tip of her nose. "We spend a lot of time talking about me. You've told me very little about yourself. Why? Is it because you don't trust me?"

Vivian broke their connection and rested her head on his chest. "I want to trust you, Alonso…"

"But you're reluctant. Is it because of your ex or your father?" The firm warning she'd given him earlier about her father had piqued his curiosity.

"My father has nothing to do with it. He was a good man, a hardworking man who loved me and my mother with his entire heart."

"Tell me about him."

Vivian was silent for a moment. "I don't want to talk about it."

When she attempted to roll off him, he held her in place. "Tell me about your father."

"Tell me about *your* father, Alonso!" Vivian closed her eyes and rubbed her hand across her forehead. "I'm sorry," she said, her tone much calmer. "I'm sorry," she repeated, opening her eyes to look at him.

"I never knew my father, Vivian. Never knew if he was a good man or a bad one. But I convinced myself it was the latter, because what kind of *man* walks out on his family, leaving the mother of his child to fend for herself? For a lot of years, I harbored so much hate toward the man who abandoned us. Then one day I realized I couldn't be angry with him because obviously no one ever taught him how to be a man."

Vivian let out a single sob, tears running down her cheeks.

"*Shit.* I didn't mean to make you cry."

"I killed my father."

Alonso stilled. "What?"

"Not physically. Emotionally. With my words."

Alonso blew a mental sigh of relief that he hadn't spent the night making love to a woman who belonged on the show *Snapped*.

"My family fell on hard times. While they worked to rebound, my father thought it would be a good idea for me to come to North Carolina and live with my grandmother for a while. My mother was against it, but…"

"She supported your father's decision."

Vivian nodded. "I was so angry at him. I just didn't realize at the time that what he was doing was for my own good."

"We never do."

"Before I left for North Carolina…" Vivian paused. "Before I left, I told my father I hated him."

Vivian's bottom lip quivered, and Alonso knew how difficult it had to be for her to tell her story.

"Every single night for two weeks he'd call to speak to his *baby girl*, but I refused to come to the phone. I was going to ignore him until he allowed me to return home. I was so stubborn as a child."

Not just as a child, he wanted to say but kept the thought to himself.

"Every night he left the same message. 'I fill your cheeks with butterfly kisses.' A week later he died of a massive heartache. I broke his heart. All he ever wanted to do was give me the world."

Vivian's body shook in his arms and he held her tight against his chest. He knew there wasn't anything he could say at the moment that would console her. So he said nothing, simply held her close, allowed her to ride out this treacherous storm and made sure she knew that he would keep her afloat.

Chapter 15

When Vivian cracked her eyes open, she couldn't believe the clock read twelve. *Twelve?* That couldn't be right. She sprang forward, immediately glancing to the space Alonso had occupied. Empty. *Where'd he...?* The sound of the shower filtered through and a smile touched her lips.

Her focus slid to the amazing view in front of her. While her room had windows that fully opened to reveal the splendor of the island, Alonso's room had a glass wall that, when fully opened, as it had been since the night before, appeared as if there was no wall at all.

A warm breeze flowed in, and Vivian inhaled the crisp air. Reclining, she recalled her and Alonso's night together. *Amazing.* She'd never made love so much in one night in her entire life. And each time trumped the last. But that hadn't been the best part. The best part had been falling asleep to the sounds of the ocean, enveloped in Alonso's arms.

Her jovial feeling faded when she recalled what had led

to that moment. She'd actually shared her pain with him. The one she'd kept locked in her heart for so long. Until the words were coming, she'd never known how much she actually needed to share her story.

A faint smile touched her lips. Alonso had urged her to share with him. He hadn't tried to convince her that she was being ridiculous. Hadn't tried to downplay her grief. Hadn't advised her to bottle her emotions. He'd simply held her so close and so tight that she felt like an extension of him. Whether she wanted to admit it or not, after last night, their relationship had taken on a whole new dynamic. It scared the hell out of her.

They were seeing each other naked. Not in the absence-of-clothes sense, but in an essence-of-who-they-really-were type of fashion. Their cloaks had fallen away, exposing each to the other's pain. She felt comfortable with him. Safe with him. Which was absolutely ridiculous.

She closed her eyes. *Please don't let it all be a game.* But after the night they'd shared, could she really believe the man she was truly seeing, for what felt like the first time, was anything but genuine? No one could have shared their feelings, bared their soul, given their energy to another the way Alonso had given himself to her without being authentic. No, the kind of connection they had shared couldn't be faked.

The bathroom door creaked open and Alonso slowly strolled out, scrubbing a towel over his hair. Another towel—dark gray and hung low—was wrapped around his waist. Vivian appreciated the sight in front of her. Especially the imprint pressing against the cotton. Even when he wasn't aroused, his manhood was impressive.

Her eyes slowly rose, raking over his damp chest, muscular arms, wide shoulders. When her gaze reached his face, he was eyeing her. A smirk lifted one corner of the sexy mouth that had brought her unparalleled pleasure most of the night and part of the morning.

"Are you checking me out?"

"Pssh. What…ever. I've seen better bodies on ragdolls." She rolled onto her stomach, turned her head away from him and snickered. A beat later, Alonso pounced on the bed and tickled her. Pinned under his solid frame, she was helpless. "Uncle, uncle, uncle!"

After several more seconds, Alonso halted his playful antics and kissed her gently on the lips. "Good morning, slash afternoon."

"Good morning, slash afternoon to you. For the record, I never sleep this late. It's all your fault." Alonso kissed the crook of her neck, causing a tingle at the spot.

"I will happily take the blame."

He snuggled next to her. They stared into each other's eyes, not uttering words for a long time. Even silence with him was pleasurable. And though they weren't speaking, the moment spoke volumes.

"Thank you, Alonso. For last night. Thank you for listening without judgment."

"You don't need to thank me. I'm just happy you trusted me with something so personal. I think we're making progress."

"Yeah, we are. You smell good. It's a turn-on."

"A turn-on, huh?" He kissed her shoulder. "What about this?" He kissed the space under her earlobe. "And this." He kissed the side of her neck. "And…" He peppered several kisses along her arm.

She laughed. "Yep, all of that works."

"What are we—" When his cell phone rang, he growled, then cursed under his breath.

That device was such a nuisance. "You better take it. It's probably work. I need to shower anyway."

He reached across to the nightstand and silenced the ringing. "Work can wait. This can't."

"It's going to have to," she said. "I have to pee."

Alonso groaned and rolled onto his back. "You're going to leave me like this?"

He pointed to the erection tenting the towel. It was such a tempting sight. But she knew if they started, it would be hours before they stopped. And to be honest, she wasn't sure she could handle any more of him right now. She needed a few hours for her body to reset itself.

Placing a kiss to his cheek, she said, "You should probably rest up. I plan to dance the night away at Music on the Green. Then later…I have even bigger plans for you." She bounced her brows twice, rolled out of bed and ambled across the floor.

"Mmm, mmm, mmm. I like what I see. You do wicked things to my body. You should probably lock the bathroom door. But I can't guarantee even that will keep me out."

Vivian laughed as she closed the door. However, she kept it unlocked just in case… Her body would just have to adjust.

Inside the bathroom, she eyed her nakedness in the mirror. Running a hand down her torso, her skin prickled. Alonso had explored every inch of her. Numerous times. The fact that he hadn't seemed to be able to get enough of her brought on a level of excitement.

The inability to get enough hadn't been one-sided. She'd been downright greedy, gobbling up every delicious inch he'd offered. Though she was quite full and satisfied now, she knew the hunger for him would soon return with a vengeance.

Alonso's voice tore into her thoughts.

"I'm starving. We polished off everything from Mama Tu's. I say we go for cheesesteaks. I'll take you to my favorite sub spot. They make the best cheesesteaks in Wilmington, hands down."

"I love cheesesteaks. If we keep eating like this, you're going to make my inner plus-size diva become my outer plus-size diva." When Alonso didn't respond, she said, "Hello?"

Still…nothing.

Finishing her business, she washed her hands and stepped back into the bedroom. Alonso was gone and so was his phone. She caught sight of him on the far end of his balcony, pacing back and forth. A sinking feeling washed over her. She hoped whatever he was discussing had nothing to do with her.

Alonso ran a hand over his head as he waited for Roth to come back on the line. What in the hell was taking him so long? He peeped through the opened balcony doors to check the bathroom door again. Still closed. Good.

"Sorry about that, man. What's up?" Roth said.

"I'm in trouble. Big trouble. This woman… She's under my skin. Way under my skin. Like way, way under my skin. I think I'm falling for her," Alonso said in a whisper. Who was he afraid would hear him, the seagulls?

Roth laughed. "So what's the problem?"

Was this man he trusted with his life laughing at him? "This shit's not funny, Ro. I expected her to have some effect on me." He sighed heavily. "But nothing like this. I'm in trouble," he reemphasized. "*Dammit.* I knew I shouldn't have spent the night with her," he said more to himself than Roth. Like he'd had any other options. His body had fiended for her. "How was I to know she would imprint on me?"

"Come again?"

"Imprint. The movie *Twilight*. The werewolf—"

"Man, I know what imprint means. I've seen the movies. What I don't know is if I heard you correctly when you said, and I quote, 'I knew I shouldn't have spent the night with her.' End quote. If I'm remembering correctly, you specifically stated you had no plans of seducing her."

Alonso tossed another quick glance inside the room. "I didn't seduce her." Okay, he kinda did, but there was no need to overshare. "Anyway, my sleeping with her is not the issue." Well, it kinda amplified the issue, but one thing at a time. Right now, trying to figure out what in the hell Vivian was doing to him held precedence.

"Sounds like love to me."

Alonso stopped so abruptly his upper body tilted forward, nearly sending him toppling over. "*Whoa!* No one said anything about love. I haven't even known her long enough to entertain a notion of love." *Love?* Was Roth insane? *Love?* Strong like, maybe. But not love. *Definitely not love.*

"My grandparents met on a Wednesday. Fell in love on Friday. Were married on Saturday. They lived in wedded bliss for fifty-two years. Anything is possible."

"Things were different in those days. Those kinds of connections don't happen anymore."

"Sorry to break it to you, man, but love is love, despite what decade it is."

Alonso mulled over Roth's words. He liked Vivian, a lot, that was for damn sure. But love? Roth's words pulled Alonso out of his thoughts.

"I'm going to venture and say your time on the island is going great."

"Better than great. There was a wrinkle, but I ironed it out. Vivian overheard a conversation with Garth about her house."

"Damn. I bet that didn't go over well."

"It got hairy for a minute, but it's all good now."

"So what now? You can't exactly go forward with the

project without her house, can you? Sounds to me like the house is no longer on your radar."

"No, but I have something else in mind. Something I think she'll appreciate. I just need to work on the logistics."

"Yeah, sounds like love to me."

Not this again. Alonso barked a laugh. Did men really talk about this type of shit? "Whatever."

After a few more minutes of small talk, Alonso ended the call. Leaning against the banister, he stared out into the water. If everyone had a view like this, there would be no need for therapists.

Enjoying the calming effects of the ocean, Roth's words haunted him. *Love?* No, his life had never been that simple. Nothing had ever come that easy for him. Especially love.

"Don't jump."

The mere sound of Vivian's voice brought a smile to his face. When he turned to face her, his words snagged. She mesmerized him in an off-the-shoulder silver sequined shirt that flashed just enough skin to stir his hunger, a pair of dark denim capri pants that hugged the curves he'd ridden all night, and a pair of sparkly open-toed sandals. "*Wow.* You look amazing."

She performed a slow turn to show off her outfit. "You like?"

"I do, I do." He wrapped his arms around her and pulled her flush against him. "Me likey a whole lot. I'm not sure I want to share you with the world today. Someone might eye you too hard, and I just might get jealous."

"Are you a jealous man, Mr. Wright?"

The seductive manner in which she said his name stirred him below the waist. "I'm a protective man, Ms. Moore."

"Huh. That's good to know. Especially since I haven't felt protected in a long while."

"I'm here now. You'll never have to feel unprotected again."

He tilted forward and kissed her tenderly. Roth's words invaded his thoughts again. This wasn't love, but damn if it didn't feel like it could be. That was far more than he was comfortable admitting. Even to himself.

Chapter 16

Vivian hadn't believed the island could get more beautiful, but she'd been wrong. The large area she'd admired when they'd first arrived had been transformed into something spectacular. Tiny string lights lit the entire space, while colored canon lights highlighted the stage. The plain white gazebo had been draped in white fabric and decorated in pink and white flowers and also outlined in tiny lights. Vivian couldn't believe how romantic the once-drab structure now looked.

The greenest lawn she'd ever seen was overflowing with people dancing, laughing and chatting, lounging in chairs, and some were snuggled up on blankets.

Several artists had already graced the raised platform, filling the large area with some of the best jazz she'd ever heard. Some performances were upbeat and a take on current hits, while others were superseductive. Those were the ones she'd taken the most pleasure in, because she'd enjoyed teasing Alonso with her sensual moves.

"If you keep grinding your ass against me like that, these people are going to get one helluva show," Alonso whispered in Vivian's ears, then kissed her lobe. "You have me hard as a rock."

She smirked and gyrated against him with even more determination.

"Woman, you are going to pay for this when we get home."

Promises, promises.

"Good to see we're not going to be the only dirty dancers here."

Vivian whipped around, embarrassment warming her cheeks. She instantly recognized the couple as the one they'd seen walking along the beach. The Jenkinses, if she remembered correctly.

"Don't stop on our account," Mrs. Jenkins said.

Alonso wrapped an arm around Vivian's waist and pulled her close to him. "Vivian Moore, please meet Mr. and Mrs. Jenkins."

The older woman waved Alonso's words off and extended her hand. "Flora," Mrs. Jenkins said. "And this is my Theodore."

When the woman glanced up at her husband, she regarded the man with so much admiration Vivian couldn't help but smile. She swore it was the most enduring thing she'd ever seen.

"'Mr. and Mrs.' You trying to make us sound old, or something?" said Theodore Jenkins.

They all laughed.

Sobering, Alonso said, "No way would anyone ever mistake you two for being old. You're the hippest couple on the island."

Theodore snapped his fingers with a loud crack, then pointed at Alonso. "You better believe it."

Vivian liked these two already.

"I know you've probably been told this already, but you two make a striking couple," said Flora.

Vivian glanced up at Alonso, the comment not giving her pause as it had previous times. "Once or twice. But thank you just the same."

Alonso regarded her with a look of esteem. It made her heart race.

"Young love," Theodore said with a hearty laugh.

The mention of love seemed to snap Alonso out of his daze. His focus drifted from her and back to Flora and Theodore.

"Um…you…you two are late on the scene. You're usually the first ones here."

Vivian could tell that Theodore's words really had Alonso rattled. She understood why. Love played no part in whatever this was they had going on. They were just having fun. She ignored the voice in the back of her head that suggested fun could easily turn into love.

Flora glanced up at her husband with adoring eyes. "We were…um…*busy*."

The two giggled like school kids who'd just been asked an embarrassing question by their teacher. Vivian loved their playful manner and the way they seemed to truly adore one another. Alonso had been right about their energy. The brief time she'd been in their presence, she'd experienced it.

"Sounds like we're bordering TMI," said Alonso.

Theodore laughed, then slid his attention to Vivian. "Mind if we camp out beside y'all? Wouldn't want to intrude or anything."

"No intrusion at all," she said. "Please join us."

Vivian could feel Alonso's eyes on her. When she glanced up at him, a corner of his beautiful mouth lifted into a half smile. He was there but not completely. What was racing through his mind—Theodore's love comment?

If so, Alonso didn't have to trouble himself with that. She wasn't under any delusions of love.

After Theodore spread the blanket, he clapped Alonso on the shoulder. "Let's check out that bar. I hope they have a better bartender this year than they had last."

Theodore's words appeared to yank Alonso out of his stupor. "Sounds good. What would you like?" he asked Vivian.

After the bottle of champagne they'd already polished off, she should have declined any more alcohol. But since it was their last night on the island, might as well live it up. "Surprise me."

"Surprise you, I shall." He planted a kiss to her lips before moving away.

Vivian and Flora lowered to their respective blankets.

"Rumor had it Alonso was on the island with someone as gorgeous as a baby doll. For once, the rumors have been accurate."

Cleary news traveled fast here. "Thank you." Curious, Vivian shifted toward Flora. "Does he bring women to the island often?"

Flora flashed an all-knowing smile. "It's been years."

Vivian attempted to mask the relief she felt, but it escaped in the form of a low-wattage smile.

"You've got yourself a good man." Flora eyed the direction their men had ventured. "Despite it not working out with him and my granddaughter, I still think the world of Alonso. He reminds me a lot of my Theo."

Granddaughter? Had Vivian heard Flora correctly? "Alonso dated your granddaughter?" When Flora eyed her, Vivian guessed the woman regretted allowing the tidbit of information to slip out.

"Yes. My granddaughter did something foolish, something unforgivable." She shook her head. "Anyway... Alonso doesn't know that I know the real reason for their split, but my granddaughter finally broke down and told me everything."

Her face contorted in what Vivian took as disgust.

"Needless to say, I was appalled. Alonso had had every right to dump her flat on her ass. No woman should ever need to trap a man. He either wants you or he doesn't. Plain and simple."

Vivian deduced that the woman who'd poked holes in the condoms and Flora's granddaughter were one and the same.

Vivian wasn't sure how she felt about the information she'd just learned. Why hadn't Alonso told her this when they'd first seen the Jenkinses walking along the beach at Mama Tu's? *Because there hadn't been a need.* At that point, they weren't even really friends.

Heck, what were they now? Friends with benefits? Lovers? Homey lover friends? She wasn't sure. They hadn't discussed it. Maybe they needed to.

Vivian spotted Alonso and Theodore headed their way, drinks in hand.

"Please keep this conversation between us, Vivian. I probably should have kept my big mouth shut about my granddaughter. I can be a real chatterbox at times."

"No, it's fine. I won't repeat a word."

Once the initial shock of what Mrs. Jenkins had told Vivian had worn off, Vivian had really enjoyed the amusing older couple. They'd spent hours talking, chatting, dancing and goofing around. When the show ended— a little after eleven—Vivian hadn't wanted to part ways with the two.

A short time later, Vivian and Alonso arrived at the house. The full moon bounced rays of brilliant light off the water, causing the waves to sparkle like jewels. As she waited for Alonso to round the vehicle to open her door, she had an idea. Exiting the Jeep, she said, "It's such a beautiful night. Let's relax on the beach awhile. It is our last night here."

"It's almost midnight, gorgeous."

"And?" Vivian walked her fingers up his chest. "Are you saying you don't want to cuddle with me in the sand, under the stars, with the sound of waves crashing? The midnight—"

"Okay, okay. I'm sold. I'll grab the blanket."

Several moments later, Vivian was positioned between Alonso's legs, her back snuggled against his warm, hard chest, his strong arms cocooned around her. It was sheer heaven.

"You were right, this was a good idea," he said, nuzzling the side of her neck.

"Told you."

"Know-it-all."

When Vivian lowered her head back and grew quiet, he jostled her playfully. "What's on your mind?"

"Nothing. It's just…" Did she really want to bring up their unknown status now? No. The moment was too perfect to disturb. "Never mind."

"Out with it."

She searched her mind for something benign to use to fill the gap she'd opened. "I was going to say it's been a while since my brain hasn't been in overdrive, thinking about a thousand things I needed to do. It's kind of nice to just live in the moment. And this is a very beautiful moment. Thank you."

"Why are you thanking me?"

"Because if it hadn't been for you inviting me—and Tressa convincing me to come," she said in a whisper, "I never would have—"

"Whoa. Your best friend convinced you to come?"

Vivian tilted her head to eye him. "Let's just say I had… *reservations* about your intent."

"Because you thought I was up to something?"

"Yes," she said plainly. "And because..." She slid her attention away from him.

"And because, what?"

"Because... I was a *wee* bit attracted to you."

Alonso barked a laugh. "Damn. I never would have guessed that."

She wasn't sure if he was being cynical or truthful.

Alonso laughed more, then asked, "And now? Do you still believe I'm up to something?"

She hoped not. "No."

He placed his hand under her chin and rotated her head toward him. "Good." Planting a delicate kiss to her lips, he said, "Very good."

His arms tightened around her again and they returned their attention to the ocean.

"Please remind me to send Tressa flowers, a necklace, a pair of diamond earrings...something to express my sincere gratitude," Alonso said.

"You are so full of it. I'm glad I got a chance to experience this serenity. So, yes, a thank-you is in order."

"In that case, you are very welcome."

Comfortable silence shrouded them again. Unfortunately, it provided a breeding ground for Vivian's inquisitiveness to spawn. "The Jenkinses are great. How long have you known them?"

"A while."

When he didn't say more—like, *I dated their granddaughter*—she experienced a hint of disappointment. "I see."

"Do you remember the ex I told you about? The one who'd wanted to get married?"

"Yes."

"She's Flora and Theo's granddaughter."

His honesty was a caress to her soul. She played clueless. "*Really?* I guess us hanging with them tonight had to be awkward, right?"

"Why would it be?"

She shrugged. "I don't know. I just…" She just what? She didn't even know. "Do you ever see her? When you come here, I mean?"

"Yes."

Vivian's body tensed. *Yes.* Was that all he was going to give her? "Oh."

Alonso squeezed her. "*Oh.* What does that mean?"

"Just…oh."

"Nothing sexual has happened between us since we split. She's here. I'm here. We keep things cordial. That's it. It shouldn't bother you."

Vivian released a clumsy laugh. "Bother me? It doesn't bother me. Why would it bother me?"

"Your body tensed when I said yes. It was faint, but I felt it."

Well, what the hell else could she say? She definitely wasn't going to admit that maybe it did bother her a little. That would suggest she didn't trust him, which she did—well, was trying to do. There would always be a minute amount of doubt floating about. Because of the betrayals she'd experienced in her past, she wasn't sure that would ever change. But she was trying. That had to mean something, right? That had to be enough.

Alonso didn't press her for a response; he simply kissed the back of her head and allowed her to hide in her silence. His endurance was one of the many things she liked about him. In an attempt to lighten the mood, she said, "Have you ever gone skinny-dipping?"

"Yes. In the lake when I was much younger."

"Let's do it."

"Let's do what?"

"Let's go skinny-dipping." Vivian peeled out of Alonso's

arms and pushed to her feet. "It'll be fun," she said, holding her hand out for him to take.

"Woman, are you insane? I'm not going out there in the dark."

Vivian backed away from him. "Suit yourself. But I'm going in. If you change your mind, you know where to find me."

She smirked, turned and walked toward the crashing waves, stripping away clothing. She would have liked to have attributed her wild behavior to the alcohol she'd consumed, but this was all her. Alonso made her feel wild, wacky and free.

As she neared the water, just one question lingered: Could Alonso truly resist her? She couldn't wait to find out.

Chapter 17

Alarm filled Alonso. "Vivian, baby— *Shit*." He ran a hand over his head. "She's really going in the water," he whispered to himself. "That's probably not a good idea. Baby, haven't you seen the movie *Jaws*? There was a scene similar to this. A woman going into the water at night. She was eaten. Down to the bone. The bone, baby, the bone."

Vivian laughed. "I'll take my chances."

Did she just— Her silhouette under the moonlight was one of the most beautiful sights he'd ever seen. With her every curve highlighted, it stirred a need in him.

"Are you afraid of some little old shark?"

Wasn't she? Obviously the champagne and sangria she'd consumed earlier had given her false bravado. Damn, if she got eaten, he'd be partially to blame. He couldn't live with that on his conscience. "Come out of the water, baby. We'll skinny-dip in the daylight. I promise."

"Quit being a chicken, Alonso Wright."

Chicken? He rested his hands on his hips and scoffed. He wasn't a damn chicken. "I'm not a chicken."

When Vivian removed her bra and panties, slinging them onto the shore, his dick instantly reacted. In that moment, she had him believing that in a battle with a bull shark, he'd come out the victor.

Stripping out of his clothes, he attempted to rationalize his impending actions. *Sharks don't even swim at night.* His brow furrowed. *Right?* He was sure he'd heard that on some Shark Week show. He paused. Hadn't he? Didn't matter. If he got gobbled up, he'd go a happy man.

Once he'd joined Vivian waist deep in the water, he pulled her into his arms. "Now, who were you calling a chicken?"

"I only used it as a persuasion tactic. And it worked."

Alonso lifted Vivian into his arms. When her legs wrapped around him, the heat of her core roused him even more. A guttural sound rumbled in his chest. Before he could claim her delicious mouth, she claimed his. She kissed him in an impatient and hungry manner, and damn if he didn't love it.

Their tongues sparred, tangled, searched. They lapped, tamed, demanded. He wanted her. Wanted her bad.

Running a hand up her wet back and along her neck, he intertwined his fingers in her hair. Tearing his mouth away, he held her gaze. Even in moonlight, he could see the desire radiating in her eyes. Did she witness in his the fact she would soon get exactly what she wanted? What they both wanted. What *he* desperately needed.

He guided her head back, then dragged his tongue along the column of her neck. The salt water had seasoned her like fine meat, making her even more appetizing. Peppering kisses to her breast, he took one of her hardened nipples into his mouth. His tongue circled. His lips sucked. His teeth nipped.

"Alonso."

He loved hearing his name roll from her lips. "Yes, baby. I'm here."

"I need it."

"And you'll get it."

"Now."

With her demand, coupled with the need to explore her more in-depth, taste her sweet essence, fill her completely, he waded through the water and headed toward shore. With Vivian still in his arms, he lowered their naked bodies onto the blanket. "You are so damn beautiful. Inside and out."

"You make me feel beautiful."

He pushed a lock of her damp hair from her face. "You're mine, Vivian Moore. I don't ever want you to allow another man to touch you in the ways I touch. You're mine. Every inch of you." When her eyes turned glossy, he prayed she wouldn't cry. Her tears were his weakness.

Vivian rested her hands on either side of his face. "Okay. But I want the same in return. I don't want to share you, Alonso."

"I'm a bull shark, dammit. But you make me feel like a powerless guppy. I don't like that shit. But at the same time, I do."

Fine lines etched Vivian's forehead. "What on earth does that mean?"

He searched her eyes. "It means I'm yours. Every inch of me."

She pulled his mouth to hers and kissed him with a gentle finesse. This time their connection was unhurried and calm. An intimate seal to their newly defined status.

The first time he'd seen her, he'd wanted her. The second time, he'd wanted her to be his. There'd never been any doubt in his mind that she'd leave the island as his. But now...now she knew it, too.

He kissed her chin, her collarbone. He kissed the valley between her breasts, then the breasts themselves. He sucked one of her diamond-hard nipples into his mouth. A soft moan floated past her lips and it let him know she enjoyed his teasing.

Kissing his way to the opposite breast, he gave it equal attention. Vivian squirmed under him. Yeah, she was ripe for the picking but he kept her on the vine a while longer. Moving lower down her body, he kissed the mound of curly dark hairs.

Instead of using his hands, he used his tongue to spread her wet folds apart. When he gently sucked her clit between his lips, Vivian cried out. In an unexpected move, she glided her hands between her legs and spread herself further apart.

Looping his arms around her thighs, Alonso inched up on his knees, bringing the lower half of Vivian's body with him. Like a wild man, he attempted to consume her whole.

She moaned.

She shrieked.

She bucked.

Then she came. Hard. So hard he felt her pulsate against his mouth.

He continued to feast on her, claiming each wave, each ripple, every drop of her essence, until her body had nothing more to offer. Returning her flat onto the blanket, he covered her body with his. "You really know how to unleash the beast in me."

He kissed her hard.

He kissed her rough.

He tried to taste her soul.

Then he pulled away. "Have you had enough of me?"

"No. I want more. So much more."

Without thinking, without considering the consequences of his actions, he entered her. The raw feel of her wrapped warm and wet around him sent an almost debilitating surge through his entire body.

Protection. He needed protection.

The warning came. The warning went.

Unable to stop himself, unable to pull out and take the necessary steps to protect them both, he delivered long, unhurried strokes. She felt too damn good to him. And she fit him. Fit him far better than any glove he'd ever worn. Fit him like a second skin. Fit him perfectly.

"You're safe," he whispered against their joined mouths. He had to let her know that he would never put her in any danger.

"I know," she said breathlessly. "So are you."

Alonso desperately fought the urge to drive himself into her untamed and impatient. But he wouldn't last beyond ten—five—strokes if he didn't take his time with her.

This hadn't been the first time he'd experienced not having a barrier between himself and his lover, but it was the first time he'd experienced anything like this. His body reacted to Vivian on a cellular level. And it felt as if a part of her was becoming a part of him in way beyond anything he'd even known.

"I can't get enough of you," he said, adjusting her leg to drive himself even deeper into her. There were no apologies made for his greed. He wanted to stay buried inside of Vivian until he physically could no longer deny his release.

Her cries taunted the ferocious hunger inside of him. Primal need kicked in. He delivered powerful strokes that dangled him on the edge of exploding. *Not yet.*

"Alonso, I'm coming. It feels so good. Oh… Oh… my—"

Vivian's head jerked and her back arched off the blanket. Alonso dragged his tongue along the column of her neck. Her fingers strangled handfuls of sand. If they went into the water now, they'd have nothing to worry about, because the piercing sound she emitted had to have frightened away any sea creature for miles.

Teeth clenched, Alonso experienced the sensations of an impending release. His strokes—though still powerful and swift in delivering—grew clumsy. Vivian's sand covered hands explored his back, and her gritty touch did him in.

A growl rumbled from deep inside of Alonso's chest as his seed spilled inside of Vivian. He came with the intensity of a geyser. Shattered, he pushed himself inside of her again and again until he couldn't manage another stroke.

His lungs burned as he snatched in breath after breath. Vivian's breathing was just as labored as his as she trembled beneath him. Still joined, she pulsed around him and he continued to twitch inside of her. The sparks of pleasure took a moment to fade.

Alonso planted a kiss on the tip of Vivian's nose before pulling out of her. He pulled her into his arms. "You were right. It is a beautiful night."

Vivian kissed his chest. "Yeah, it is."

Something about her tune troubled him. Alonso lifted slightly, placed a finger under her chin, and tilted her head so that he was looking into her eyes. "Are you okay?"

"Perfect."

He eyed her intently. "Are you sure?"

A smile curled her lips. "Yes." She lowered her head back to his chest.

Alonso stared up at the stars. The way Vivian made him feel scared him. He'd hid from her, locked his true self away—a simple man who just wanted to be happy. Somehow, she'd found him. And now she had something of his that he'd always fervently guarded. She had his heart.

When Vivian eased out of Alonso's arms, he rustled a bit but didn't wake. He definitely had a right to be exhausted. It'd been close to three in the morning when they'd ventured in from the beach. It was barely six now. She, on the other hand, hadn't slept a wink.

Inching out of the bed, she slid into her oversize nightshirt, grabbed her phone and headed out the open balcony door. Outside, she followed the stairs down to the beach. The sun hadn't made it over the horizon, but the faint light from its approach lit the sky in a peachy, yellow, orange hue.

This island had put her at peace the moment she'd arrived. But even the grandeur of it wasn't enough to calm the sea of emotions raging inside of her now.

Tapping in Tressa's number, she waited for her to answer.

Tressa's groggy voice came over the line. "Vi? Is everything okay?"

"No. I'm in trouble."

Tressa's tone livened. "I'm putting on my shoes right now. Text me the address."

Another reason why she loved her best friend. The woman never hesitated to come to her aid. Vivian laughed. "Not that kind of trouble, Tress."

"So… I'm not coming to kick anyone's ass?"

"No." Though maybe Vivian needed some sense kicked into hers.

"Clearly, something's wrong."

Vivian tossed a glance toward the house. "Well, other than the fact I'm about one hundred and fifteen percent sure I'm falling in love with Alonso, nothing." But wasn't that plenty?

Vivian pulled the phone away from her ear when Tressa squealed loud enough to shatter glass. No doubt Tressa thought Vivian's revelation was a good thing and celebration-worthy. Too bad Vivian didn't.

"I knew you two were going to fall in love. I sensed it.

I'm never wrong about these things. The aura around the two of you is so powerful."

Vivian ambled along the shore, frothy waves lapping at her feet. "This is not a good thing, Tress. It's…" This had to be the worst thing that could have happened. There was no room in her life for love, for false promises, for disappointment. She sighed heavily. "You're not supposed to cheer. You're supposed to tell me how insanely foolish I am for falling in love with a man I barely know."

"Why would I tell you something silly like that?"

Now that Vivian thought about it, maybe a woman who'd gotten engaged four months after meeting her now fiancé was perhaps not the best person to use as a love deterrent. "How did this happen?" she said more to herself than Tressa. "It's this damn romantic, angelic, magical island." She kicked wet sand for effect.

"It doesn't matter why it happened. It happened. Embrace it. It's love, Vi. Fall. Fall hard."

"It's not the falling part that scares me. It's the not being caught." Yes, Alonso had made her feel like his, made her feel safe, made her feel secure, but her life had been an example of Murphy's Law. In her mind, something was bound to go wrong.

Tressa's tone grew tender. "He'll catch you. Trust that."

"And if he doesn't?"

"Quit that, Vi. Trust your heart. The heart knows. It knows how to hurt. It knows how to heal. It knows when it's ready to love again. And your heart is ready, sis."

Vivian dug her big toe into the sand. Well, she was glad someone could see all of this inside of her, because she wasn't sure she could. The only thing she was sure of was the feelings she had for Alonso. "We spent the night making love on the beach. It was so beautiful that I can't even put the experience into words." Recalling their night together caused a warm sensation to flutter through her. "What we shared last night was so powerful it scared me."

"Yep. It's love. And instead of continuing to fight it, embrace it. Now get off this phone and go cuddle with your man."

"Thank you for listening."

"What are best friends for? I'm so happy for you, Vi. You deserve every ounce of happiness you're experiencing. Not all us are fortunate enough to find such a connection."

"Is everything okay, Tress? With you and Cyrus, I mean."

"Yes. Yes, everything is fine. Now go love your man."

"Yes, ma'am. I love you."

"And you know I love you back."

Ending the call, Vivian wrapped herself in her arms and stared out at the miles and miles of water, renewing itself with every fresh wave that crashed along the shoreline. The ocean made things seem so easy.

"Don't tell me you're watching the sunrise without me? I'd be hurt."

The sound of Alonso's voice startled her. Swallowing the myriad of emotions crashing through her, she turned to face him. The sight of him took her breath away. Barefoot, bare chested and wearing a pair of thin white pajama bottoms that hung tantalizingly low, and no underwear. Shaking away the instant arousal, she said, "You were sleeping so peacefully. I didn't want to wake you."

In reach, Alonso cradled her face between his hands. Staring into her eyes, he said, "Good morning, beautiful," then kissed her as if he'd longed for years to taste her forbidden mouth.

Once the kiss ended, he guided her away from the water and lowered her onto the sand, directing her between his legs, her back against his chest. Once in place, he wrapped her tightly in his embrace and kissed the side of her neck. It sent shivers up her spine.

Vivian rested her head against him. "Have you ever seen anything more beautiful?"

"Yes." He kissed her shoulder. "When I watched you from the balcony, your hair blowing in the wind." He kissed her neck again. "The waves lapping at your feet, worshipping you like the goddess you are."

"You are quite the poet."

"You are quite the inspiration."

"I was talking to Tressa." She felt the need to tell him that. In case he had any other ideas.

Alonso didn't respond. He lifted her hand, flipped it over and kissed the tulip tattoo there. "If your grandmother were here, I'd hug her and say thank you."

Vivian's brow furrowed. "Thank you? For what?"

"For raising a woman like you."

Her heart swelled and wrapped snuggly around the idea of loving Alonso, which suddenly no longer seemed so overwhelming. Looming tears burned her eyes, and her voice cracked as she spoke. "That was a very kind thing to say."

Alonso directed her head toward him. "I can't be your father, Vivian, but I *can* give you the world. And I will if you allow me, along with all of the butterfly kisses you can handle."

Tears rolled down her cheeks. Beautiful things just kept flowing past his lips. She responded with the only answer that made sense. "Okay." And quietly allowed herself to love the man who wanted to give her the world.

Chapter 18

For the first time ever, Alonso hated being in the office. Like really hated being in the office. Ever since he'd returned from Infinity Island two weeks ago, work no longer brought the same fulfillment. What brought him fulfillment now? Spending time with Vivian. He was a different man when he was with her. A patient, less intimidating man. A good and a bad thing, he reasoned.

He lifted the picture he'd taken of Vivian on the beach before they'd left the island. With his finger, he traced her image. How in the hell had he allowed himself to fall this hard for her? He laughed. He never really stood a chance. One look into those innocent eyes and he'd been a goner right there in Tender Hearts's hallway. Roth was right. He was in love with her.

Returning the frame to its resting place on his desk, he scrubbed his hands down his face. Why did loving this woman bring him so much joy, but also bother him so much at the same time? Was it because love made him vulnerable? Because love altered him? Because he'd loved and lost too many times?

Yeah, that was it. Because he'd loved and lost too many times to fully trust the emotion. His mother. His grandfather.

"Too late now," he mumbled. There was nothing he could do about it now. Vivian was embedded in him.

Alonso sighed and checked his watch again. Garth should have been there over an hour ago. It wasn't like the man to be fashionably late. Maybe he was stuck at one of his job sites. He had several high-rises being constructed. Since their last meeting hadn't gone so well, he wasn't sure whether the man would actually show at all.

When he'd told Garth about his plans of altering the original concept of the downtown Raleigh project, Alonso could tell Garth hadn't been fully supportive of the idea. And though Garth hadn't outwardly voiced his objections, Alonso had seen the disdain on his face. Plus, Garth's cold stare had nearly frozen Alonso solid.

Alonso hoped today he'd be able to convince Garth that, though this venture wouldn't be as financially rewarding as the original plan, it would still net a good profit for him, since money seemed to always persuade him. If not, they'd have to simply part ways gracefully, because there was no changing Alonso's mind about this. There would be no better way to honor his grandfather *and* the woman he loved.

He smiled thinking about how stunned Vivian would be when he told her about the new venture. *Soon.*

"Mr. Wright?"

His assistant's voice boomed over the speaker.

"Yes, Jessica?"

"The mayor, city manager and Mr. Major from the planning department have all confirmed for next month."

Alonso pumped his fist into the air. One step closer to completing his puzzle. "Thank you for letting me know."

"And Mr. Garrison is on his way back to see you."

Finally. "Great."

When Garth entered, Alonso could still feel the tension. Plus, Garth didn't display his usual enthusiasm. Alonso offered his hand. "I thought you'd stood me up."

"Sorry about that. I had some business to take care of," Garth said drily.

Alonso directed Garth toward the revised 3-D table model. "Here it is. The new downtown Raleigh project. In place of shops and restaurants, several transition homes to help our brothers and sisters who are trying to get back on their feet." He pointed across the display. "A youth-slash-community-slash-workforce-skills center, a day care facility and possibly even a clinic." Establishing the clinic would be the most difficult part.

Garth studied the layout, then nodded as if it didn't seem like such a bad idea after all. Was Alonso finally getting through to the man? Alonso led the way across the room, taking a seat behind his desk. Garth eased down into the chair across from him.

"I have a meeting with city officials next month to pitch the revitalization project and hopefully garner their support."

Garth's expression remained emotionless. When he propped his elbows on the arms of the chair, then intertwined his fingers under his chin, Alonso had doubts that he was getting through to the man, after all. Well, if Garth wasn't interested in moving forward with him, he'd find someone who was.

Alonso decided to try to appeal to him on a compassion level. "This project can change lives here, Garth. Give hope where there has never been much. This project won't make us rich, but it will enrich our souls. And, hey, that's—"

"That's bullshit is what it is. To *hell* with enriching my soul. Cold, hard cash enriches my soul." Garth pushed to his feet. "Who the hell are you? The Alonso Wright *I* know couldn't give a damn about enriching a soul. Where the hell is that ruthless businessman? That's the one I want to talk to. The one who is about that money."

Alonso studied Garth. Was this the same man who'd been big brother to several young men, spearheaded back-to-school supply drives, distributed turkeys to families during the holiday? Obviously this just wasn't going to work for either of them. "Garth, I understand if you want to back out of this project—"

"*Back out?* Hell, I was never in it." He jabbed his finger toward the table. "I never agreed to be a part of that shit. I build skyscrapers. Large damn construction. Not some damn dinky houses and community centers."

Spittle flew from Garth's mouth as he spoke. Alonso's eyes slid to the picture of Vivian. It put him in his calm place. In business, he always preferred to keep his cool. Plus, he didn't like to burn bridges. Until now, he and Garth had always had a great working relationship.

Garth followed Alonso's stare. "Oh, I get it now. Obviously you two explored more than business. Was this her idea?"

Vivian had no idea about Alonso's revised plans. He didn't plan on telling her until after the meeting with the mayor. But he didn't reveal any of this to Garth. Mainly because it was none of his damn business. Alonso stood. "We're done here, Garth."

"The hell we are." Garth swept his hand across Alonso's desk, sending pencils, pens and other items sailing across the room.

Before he'd realized it, Alonso had reached across the desk, snatched Garth by the collar and yanked him forward. "What the hell is wrong with you, man?"

Garth flashed his palms. "I'm sorry. I'm sorry. I lost

my cool. It's been a rough week. I didn't mean to take my frustration out on you. We're cool."

Slowing, Alonso released his grip, then chastised himself for not having better control. "You need to leave."

Garth ironed his hand down his ruffled shirt, then gave a starched nod.

Once the man exited, Alonso dropped down into his chair. What in the hell had just happened? After a minute or so of tossing the question around in his head and finding no logical explanation for Garth's behavior, he tidied his office, then decided he needed some fresh air.

Thirty minutes later, Alonso entered Hamilton's place. Clearly, he was just in time. The delicious aromas swirling made his stomach growl. If Alonso didn't know any better, he'd swear Ham had a woman around. The place was spotless.

"What's wrong with you, youngster? You look like you asked for no mayo and they slathered on double. *Ta-hee-hee.*"

Alonso massaged the back of his neck. "Rough day at the office."

"Well, why did you come here? You should have gone to that pretty lady of yours. I'm sure she's better equipped at helping you work out the kinks. *Ta-hee-hee.*"

No doubt Vivian would make him feel much better. But there was nothing she could do right now. Especially with her being in Atlanta for a conference. Damn, he couldn't wait until she returned. "She's out of town. She'll be back on Friday." *Three long days to go.*

"Lord, I know you're miserable."

Alonso chuckled, but didn't say anything.

"Well, I got something that might help. Now, it's not as lovely as the warm touch of a woman, but it'll sho' put a smile on your face."

Ham led the way into the kitchen. When they entered

the spacious room, Alonso's mouth fell open. "Uh, Ham? Where'd all this food come from?"

"Well, since I don't have to spend all day collecting cans, I gotta do something with my time. Been watching this cooking channel. They don't show a lot of soul food cooking, but some of this stuff ain't half-bad."

Alonso scanned the table: desserts, meats, seafood, breads, pastas, sauces and a few things he wasn't sure how to label. Sobering, he said, "You're trying to get me killed. And if Vivian finds out you're eating all of these cakes and pies and breads...you're a dead man, too."

A look of alarm spread across Hamilton's face and Alonso had to bite back a laugh. Vivian had already warned them both about being mindful of what Hamilton consumed, because of his diabetes. She appeared to care about Hamilton's well-being just as much as Alonso did. Just another reason he had to love her.

And Hamilton seemed taken with Vivian, too. Just like that, she'd convinced him to see the dentist and trim his hair. Something Alonso hadn't been able to do in years.

"You better not tell her," Hamilton said.

"I gotta tell her, Ham. I'm not good at hiding stuff from her." Except his feelings. "That woman can read me like a book." Which probably meant she already knew he was in love with her.

"Snitches get stitches, young blood."

"Well, if you hadn't committed the crime—" Alonso swept his hand around the room "—you wouldn't need an alibi, old man."

Hamilton burst out laughing. "*Ta-hee-hee.* Okay, okay. We'll just wrap up the not-so-good-for-you stuff. That'll work, right?"

Alonso thought for a moment, then nodded. He could support that. "Ham, this is a lot of food. What are you going to do with what we don't eat? You'll never finish all of this by yourself." Or by the time Vivian got back to town.

"Well, what we don't eat I'm going to take down to Moore Square and share it. That'll mean a few won't have to go hungry or dig through the trash for dinner tonight." A hint of sadness spread across Hamilton's face.

To hear those words escape from Hamilton's mouth broke Alonso's heart. He hated to imagine Ham ever having to Dumpster dive for food. And if he had, Alonso hoped the man knew he'd never have to again.

Well, this explained the recent increase in Hamilton's credit card bill.

"Roll up your sleeves and dig in," Hamilton said.

Alonso didn't need to be told twice. The two men feasted like kings for the next hour. Turned out Hamilton was a pretty good cook. He could give Mama Tu a real run for her money. When they returned to the living room, Alonso slouched down in the sofa. He was so full he was actually miserable. Loosening his tie, he unfastened the top button of his shirt.

Hamilton sat in his oversize brown leather recliner, the only piece of furniture he'd specifically requested. "Now, don't you feel better?"

"I feel better, but I ate too much."

"*Ta-hee-hee.* Take a nap. You'll feel better when you wake up."

"I wish I could take a nap, but I need to get back to the office." He reconsidered the words. "Actually…I don't. Being the boss has some perks." He shot a quick message to his assistant informing her he wouldn't be returning, then stashed his phone back in his pocket, reclined his head and closed his eyes.

"So you say pretty lady won't be back for a few days."

Alonso wasn't sure whether or not Ham actually remembered Vivian's name, because he always called her *pretty lady*. It always brought a toothy smile to her face. "Yeah. I can't wait."

"You love her."

Alonso wasn't sure if it was a question or a statement. His head rose slowly, and he eyed Hamilton. "Yeah, I do."

"She's good for you. And the two of you look good together. You gon' ask her to marry you?"

Alonso chuckled. "We're nowhere near that stage yet, Ham."

"Well, you should. There's something special about that one. Can't quite put my finger on it. But special, nonetheless."

Alonso had to agree with him there. Vivian was something special. And he was crazy about her.

Vivian smiled when her tablet chimed, indicating an incoming video call. *Alonso*. She swiped her finger across the screen to make the connection active. When Alonso's face filled her screen, she grew even more homesick. Odd, because she used to live for this annual nursing convention—meeting new people, discovering innovative equipment. Now all she wanted to do was jump through her device and into Alonso's arms.

"Hi, handsome."

"Hey, beautiful. Were you busy?"

"Never too busy for you."

"How's San Diego?"

"Not the same without you, but it's nice. My room overlooks the marina and the San Diego Bay. However, it's nothing in comparison to the view I had on Infinity Island."

"I wish I was in San Diego with you."

"So do I. I—" Vivian paused when there was a tap at her door.

"Is there another man coming to see you, woman? Don't make me come to San Diego."

Alonso punctuated his words with a laugh and she joined in.

"It's probably room service. I'll be right back."

"I'll be right here."

Inching off the bed, she made her way to the door.

"Find out who it is before you open the door," Alonso called out.

"Yes, sir." The sexy chuckle Alonso released sent a sensation up her spine. "Who is it?" she sang for his amusement.

"Front desk," the masculine voice called from the opposite side.

Verifying her visitor through the peephole, Vivian eased the door open. A crystal vase crammed with fresh flowers greeted her. "Oh, my goodness."

"Good evening, Ms. Moore. These are for you. Please allow me to place them. They are quite heavy."

Judging by the vast amount of stems sprouting from the vase, she was sure it was like carrying lead. She stepped aside and allowed him entry. She scrutinized the arrangement. "Wow. Thank you."

"You are very welcome." The young man turned and started away.

"Wait. Tip."

He flashed his palm. "No need. It has all been taken care of." A beat later, he disappeared through the door.

Vivian inhaled the fragrant scent wafting from the mix of lilies, roses, calla lilies, hydrangeas and, of course, tulips. Returning to a waiting Alonso, she beamed at him.

"Why do you look so happy?"

"Because I have the best man in the world, and he always knows how to make my day so much brighter."

"He sounds like a keeper to me."

"Oh, he's definitely a keeper. Thank you. I love them."

"You're welcome. Just wanted you to know that, despite us being hundreds of miles apart, you are still on my mind."

"God, I lo—*look* forward to coming home." Had she really almost told Alonso she loved him? That would have been bad. Real bad. No, it wouldn't have been. It would have been the truth, and the truth was supposed to set you free.

But did she really want to tell him over an internet connection? No. Shifting the direction of the conversation, she dragged her finger across the screen as if she could actually feel Alonso's warm skin under her fingertips. "You look tired. Long day?"

"You can say that."

"Want to talk about it?"

He scrubbed his hand over his head. "I had to sever ties with an old business associate."

"Oh, no. I'm sorry." She came off the bed again and headed toward the balcony, bringing Alonso with her. "I'll show you something that'll cheer you up."

A roguish smile spread across his face. "I'm all eyes."

"Down, boy. It's not that type of party."

"Oh, but it can be." He winked.

Vivian rotated the view of the camera and panned the marina, the countless boats docked below, the gentle ripple of the water, the twinkle of the lights in the distance. "Beautiful, right?"

"Yes. I feel better already."

Vivian eased into one of the balcony chairs and changed the direction of the camera so that Alonso was now seeing her again. "I can't wait to come home. California is nice, but my heart is in North Carolina." There. She'd partially put her feelings out there. She awaited Alonso's response.

Alonso rubbed the side of his face as if she'd reached through the screen and slapped him. "Really?"

Really? Was that all he had to say? A tiny voice in her head screamed: *You're an idiot, Vivian Moore.* She had to agree. In an attempt to clean up the statement, she said, "North Carolina is where I spent most of my life, where my best memories are. So, yeah, my heart is definitely there."

"Yeah, memories are important."

Man, she wanted to forget the last five minutes of this conversation. Definitely the segment where she'd made a complete fool of herself and practically confessed her love to only get a *really*.

Okay, maybe she was being a bit melodramatic. She hadn't exactly confessed anything. And hey, even if Alonso didn't feel the same way about her as she felt about him, so what? She enjoyed spending time with him. And at this stage of their relationship, did it truly matter whether or not he was in love with her?

Alonso cut into her thoughts and she refocused on their conversation. "I'm sorry, what did you say?"

"I asked if you had plans Saturday evening."

"Why do you ask?"

"Because I would love to take you on a date."

Shaking off whatever Alonso's one-word response meant—or hadn't meant—she smiled. "I think I'm free." One thing she couldn't deny was how much she loved their date nights. They always ended so sinfully deliciously.

"Good."

Shifting her thoughts and the conversation, she said, "Did you call Hamilton today to make sure he's checking his blood sugar like I showed him?"

"Um, yeah. Yes. I spent the afternoon with him, actually."

"That's great. What did y'all do?"

"Um, we watched a little TV. Ate. Hung out."

Alonso turned his head and scratched an itch on his neck she was sure wasn't there. He was hiding something, and she had a good idea it had something to do with Hamilton and junk food. Since he looked stressed enough, she didn't interrogate him.

"I know you're probably tired. I'll let you get some rest. I have several things to take care of before I can get out of here," he said.

She'd been so consumed with him she hadn't paid attention to his surroundings. His brown leather office chair came into view. "You're still in the office? It's almost eight."

"I'm headed out soon." The jovial expression on Alonso's face morphed into a stern one. "I miss you, Vivian. Like, *really* miss you. I can't wait to hold you in my arms. Sweet dreams, baby."

She touched the screen, desperate to say *I love you* and eager to get his response. Instead, she said, "Sweet dreams to you."

When Vivian ended the call, her heart smiled. Though he hadn't said the words, in that moment, in the depths of his dark gaze, the severity of his expression and words, she knew she wasn't loving alone.

Chapter 19

The second his eyes landed on Vivian in her little black dress, Alonso reconsidered date night. The slinky, off-the-shoulder fabric hugged her dangerous curves. The mere thought of ripping her out of it made him hard.

His admiration didn't stop at the dress. Her exposed legs did it for him, too. And he definitely approved of the strappy black stilettos she wore. She was coming out of that dress but could leave the shoes on.

Stepping inside from the porch, he said, "Oh, we are definitely staying in tonight."

Vivian held up a manicured finger. "After the week I've had, *someone* is taking me out. I need to decompress. From my delayed flight, from my canceled flight, from my lost luggage, from a crying baby, from the snoring old man who used my shoulder as a pillow and holder for his dentures."

She folded her arms across her chest and pouted play-fully before turning her back to him and stomping her heel against the hardwood.

"Okay, okay." He chuckled. "You deserve to be wined, dined and pampered." He wrapped his arms around her from behind. "And I can't wait to get to the pampering part." He kissed her neck. "All. Night. Long."

When he ground against her, she moaned. "Stop teasing me."

"Teasing you? I'm not teasing you. *This* is teasing you." He slid his hand down the front of her dress and rolled her taut nipple between two fingers. Vivian squirmed under his touch. Looked as if they would be staying in after all. "You like that?" he whispered into her ear.

Her tone was sultry when she spoke. *"Yes."*

His free hand glided along her rib cage. "I'm starving for you. I want to taste you before we leave. Can I taste you, baby?"

"Yes."

"Yeah?"

"Yes, yes, yes…*no*." She did a quick move and was out of his grasp. "Quit that, Alonso Wright."

He neared her. "Quit what?"

Backing away, she said, "You know what."

When her back collided with a wall, he rested his forearm against the space above her head and pressed his body against hers. "Kiss me."

"No. You're being a bad boy. I don't reward bad boys."

"You better kiss me, woman, before I wither up and die."

Vivian's beautiful lips curled into a lazy smile. "Are you suggesting my kisses give you life?"

"I'm not merely suggesting it. It's a fact."

Reaching up, she straightened his tie. A second later, she wrapped the red fabric around her hand and pulled him close. "I certainly don't want to be responsible for your demise. I kinda like you."

And he kinda liked her, too. Alonso crashed his mouth

to hers. Like a hungry bear preparing for hibernation, he consumed as much of her through the kiss as he could. Their connection was sweet and gave him the boost of energy he needed.

He loved and feared this woman. Why he loved her was obvious. She was selfless, kindhearted and adorably independent. He feared her because she had the power to destroy him. She made him vulnerable.

Vivian pressed her hands into his chest and inched him away, but yanked him back for one more peck. "Let's go, lover."

She slid from between the rock and the hard place he'd put her in and neared the door. His eyes fixed to her swaying ass. If it were possible to die from raw need, his lifeless body would be sprawled across her living room floor. The mortician would have to break his dick to get it down. He shook his head. "*Coming*, dear."

Oh, how he wished that were true.

Vivian loved everything about the Underground Jazz House: the food, the atmosphere, the music. Especially the music. In her opinion, the establishment employed the absolute best musicians in the state. Settling in a booth, Vivian thought about the last time she'd been there, two weeks or so ago.

It was supposed to have been a double date with Vivian, Alonso, Tressa and her fiancé, Cyrus. But at the last minute, Cyrus had called to say he wouldn't be joining them because of a work emergency. Roth had filled in for Cyrus and the four of them had had an amazing time. Had she not known any better, Vivian would have sworn that when Roth had taken to the stage that night, he'd been serenading Tressa with his saxophone. And had she *really* not known any better, she'd have sworn sparks had flown between Roth and Tressa.

Vivian laughed at herself. She'd read too much into it. She simply liked the idea of her best friend dating Alonso's best friend.

Vivian took in her surroundings. All the walls in the room were lined with satiny red fabric and washed in soft light. Tables and black leather booths reserved for VIPs were placed throughout the room. A single candle flickered on each table, while scantily lit chandeliers dangled from the ceiling.

A portly man in a tux sat behind the grand piano on the elevated stage playing a sensual tune, while an attractive woman—early forties if Vivian had to guess—was perched atop the elegant instrument, singing her heart out.

Vivian leaned in and whispered in Alonso's ear, "I feel like I've gone back in time. I love it here."

Alonso draped his arm around her shoulder, pulled her closer to him and placed a delicate kiss on her lips. Resting his forehead against hers, he said, "I need to tell you something. I l—"

"Alonso Wright?"

The shift in Alonso's demeanor was instant, the smile melting from his face. He turned his attention to the towering man who'd approached their table. When Alonso's jaw tightened, Vivian came to the conclusion that whoever this man was, Alonso wasn't too thrilled to see him.

"Garth."

When Alonso offered his hand, Vivian noticed a brief moment of hesitation from this Garth character. Obviously there was some tension between the two men, but they both played cordial. What was the animosity all about?

A mix between a smirk and scowl spread across Garth's face when he slid his attention to her. She was a 100 percent sure she hadn't done anything to the man to warrant such regard.

"Alonso, aren't you going to introduce me to this lovely lady?"

Vivian stuck out her hand before Alonso could respond. Hopefully, the quicker she acquainted herself, the sooner their unwanted visitor would disappear. "Vivian Moore. It's a pleasure to meet you."

"The pleasure is all mine."

Inwardly, she groaned when he pressed a kiss to the back of her hand. To make things worse, the clammy feel of his hand made her want to gag. *Gross.* Garth held on to her hand far longer than Vivian deemed necessary. Apparently, Alonso thought the same.

Drily, Alonso gave Garth a prompt to leave. "Enjoy the rest of your evening, Garth."

Garth flashed a lopsided smile, then finally released her hand. She slid her hand under the table and casually wiped it over the leather seat, hoping it would absorb the bad vibes she'd felt from the man.

"You do the same," Garth said to Alonso, then ambled away.

Alonso eyed Garth until the man disappeared in the darkness.

In an attempt to lighten the mood, Vivian said, "A friend of yours?" She laughed, but Alonso remained stone-faced.

"Remember the business associate I told you about?"

"The one you had to sever ties with?"

"Yeah. That was him."

Now it made sense. At least Garth had had enough decorum not to show out in a public place. Vivian took Alonso's hand into hers and squeezed. "Are you okay?" It was clear the encounter had bothered him. If she recalled correctly, the two had worked together for a while. Having to end things had to be difficult for him.

"I'm good." One corner of his mouth lifted into a lazy smile.

Vivian disliked the troubled expression on his face. They were there to have a good time and that Garth jerk had upset their harmony. Placing her hand on his cheek, she said, "Don't let him ruin our evening."

"I'm here with you. The evening could never be ruined."

He kissed her in a way that had the lighting not been so dim would have drawn every eye in the place.

"If you two need some privacy, there's an empty office in the back."

Vivian and Alonso laughed against their joined mouths, then broke their connection to face Alonso's best friend, Roth. Eyeing Roth, Vivian understood the twinkle that had sparkled in Tressa's eyes when she and Roth had first met. Like Alonso, Roth was a handsome man. Six-four, skin as rich and smooth as perfectly poured fudge, and sturdy. And also like Alonso, very successful. Why in the hell was he still single?

"Hi, Roth," Vivian said.

Roth leaned forward and placed a kiss on her cheek.

"Watch it now," Alonso said, standing to greet Roth.

The two grabbed each other in a manly embrace. They reminded her so much of her and Tressa. Inseparable.

Roth pointed over his shoulder. "I'm about to head out for a while, but Dolly will take good care of you two."

"You're not performing tonight?" asked Alonso.

"Nah. I have something to take care of."

Alonso eyed him curiously. Then, as if a light flicked on, he smiled. "All right. Well, be safe."

Considering the stern warning, Alonso must have assumed whatever Roth was getting into had something to do with a woman. When Roth ambled away, Alonso slid back in the booth.

"You think Roth has a date?" she asked.

Alonso shrugged. "Who knows?"

Vivian laughed to herself. "Men and their bro code."

As if she could sense eyes on her, Vivian scanned the room. In the distance, Garth stood, arms folded across his chest, staring directly at them. Even with the absence of quality lighting, the scowl on his face was pronounced. Something about the display made her shiver.

Alonso rubbed her arm. "Are you cold?"

Vivian faced Alonso briefly. When she tossed another glance in the direction she'd spied Garth, the man was gone. Eyeing Alonso again, she smiled. "Just a chill. I'm fine."

She snuggled close to Alonso and rested her head on his shoulder. Instead of focusing on Garth—a man that, after only knowing him a matter of minutes, she did not like—she placed all of her focus on the man she loved.

However, she just couldn't shake the uneasy feeling Garth's presence had given her.

Chapter 20

Alonso wanted to focus on simply enjoying his time with Vivian, but seeing Garth had shifted his entire mood. As hard as he'd tried, he hadn't quite been able to get back to his happy place. The man was going to be trouble. Alonso could feel it in his bones.

Pulling into Vivian's driveway, he popped the gearshift into Park and just sat there.

Vivian smoothed a hand down his arm. "I enjoyed tonight."

He captured her hand and kissed her palm. "So did I."

"You seem distracted."

A forced smile lit his expression. "I'm here. And when we get inside I'll show just how here I am."

"Promises, promises."

"You should know by now how good I am at fulfilling them." He smirked, then exited the vehicle.

On the walk to the passenger's side, he gave himself a pep talk. *Get yourself together, Wright.* When Vivian swung her leg out, the glimpse of thigh he got soothed him. Walking a few steps ahead of him, he took pleasure in the view. The sway of her hips pushed everything to the back burner. Oh, he had plans for her body.

Vivian stopped. "Huh."

His eyes crawled up her frame. "What?"

"Nothing. It's just…I thought I left the lights on."

His attention slid to the darkened windows. So did he. He rested his hands on her waist and inched her back. "Hang back a second."

"Okay."

Taking her keys, he climbed the stairs, unlocked the door and slowly inched it open. He swore he sensed movement but chalked it up to his mind playing tricks on him. His hand searched the wall for the light switch. Finding it, he flicked it on and jolted from the sight in front of him.

"Surprise!" Vivian said from behind him.

Amused and confused, he chuckled. He scrutinized the colorfully decorated room. A rainbow array of balloons bobbed all around the space. Streamers were draped from one corner of the room to the other, the colors coordinating with the balloons.

Vivian stood next to him. "It's your birthday party."

"My birthday party? You're a few months too late, or early, depending on how you look at it."

"I know, but you shouldn't have to wait any longer for a birthday party."

Before he could respond, the sounds of a saxophone radiated from the kitchen. A second later, Roth entered the room, performing the birthday song. Behind him, Tressa carried a birthday cake with one single candle stuck in the center.

Alonso's cheeks hurt from smiling so hard. He glanced over at Vivian, who appeared to be enjoying the moment just as much as he was. This woman was amazing.

When Roth finished, Alonso and Vivian applauded.

"So this is why you had to run off?" Alonso said, clapping Roth on the shoulder. He faced Tressa. "Did you bake this?" Vivian had told him Tressa was a heck of a baker and taught cooking classes in her free time.

"Absolutely. Do you think my BFF would have gotten you some meager store-bought cake?"

"No, she would not," Vivian answered.

Alonso wrapped his arms around Vivian and rocked her from side to side. "You're amazing."

Vivian beamed. "I know, right."

Staring into Vivian's eyes, everyone else in the room disappeared. He said nothing, did nothing, just stared at her, their energy more powerful than it'd ever been.

"Okay. I think our job here is done. We're going to get out of here and let you two have some privacy. It looks like you're going to need it," Tressa said. "We'll let ourselves out."

Their departures drew Alonso and Vivian's attention away from each other.

"Thank you guys for everything. I owe you both," Vivian said.

"So do I," Alonso added.

"Seeing you two so happy is payment enough," Roth said, giving Alonso a pound.

Tressa agreed, taking Vivian in a warm hug. Tressa whispered something in Vivian's ears, but Alonso couldn't make out what it was. Whatever the woman had said made Vivian grin from ear to ear.

The second Roth and Tressa exited and the door clicked closed, Alonso pulled Vivian into his arms and kissed her with urgent need. Pulling away, he eyed her intently, firmly. "You caught my eye the first time I saw you. I never imagined you'd captured my heart. I freaking love you, woman."

Vivian's cheeks mushroomed. "Oh, yeah?"

"Oh...yeah."

"Well, I freaking love you, too, man."

Vivian cradled his head in her hands and scrutinized him, her eyes roaming over every inch of his face. When a tear rolled down her cheek, it hit him like a fist to the chest. "What's wrong?"

She smiled, more tears streaming down her face. "I never wanted to fall in love with you. Heck, I never even wanted to like you. But you made it impossible not to like you. Made it impossible not to love you."

He slid the pad of his thumb across her cheek. "You should know by now that you never stood a chance."

Vivian's expression turned stern. "Loving you scares me, Alonso. The way I love you scares me. I dated a man for two years and never came close to feeling for him what I feel for you. And I don't know why you affect me this way, but you do."

"You're not the only one rattled. I'll be the first to tell you I've never been lucky with love. But I feel pretty damn fortunate to have you. Love is a risk. One I'm taking full speed ahead, because I prefer to risk it all *with* you than without you."

He scooped her into his arms and headed toward the bedroom. The need to make love to her was overwhelming. Inside, they wasted no time getting undressed. After a sensual tussle for power, he gave in and allowed Vivian to take control.

On his back, he closed his eyes and enjoyed the feel of her warm kisses trailing down his body. When she took him into her mouth, he sucked in a sharp breath, then released it in a throaty moan.

Vivian's head bobbed up and down, taking him in and out of her mouth with a slow, steady rhythm. Tangling his fingers in her hair, he moved his hands to her tempo. "It feels too good. You have to stop before I explode."

The words fell on deaf ears, because Vivian continued her magnificent torture. He visualized trees, imagined riding a roller coaster—something he hated—forced his mind to go blank. Nothing helped. He was coming.

His fingers splayed in an attempt to not snatch out locks of her hair. She gripped him tight and stroked him fast. Then it happened. He called her damn name. "Vi…vian. Oh, shit!" He roared as his seed spilled over her hands, the pressure of the release causing warm spurts to land on his stomach.

It only took the thought of driving himself deep inside of Vivian to get him hard again within seconds. In a swift motion, he had her pinned to the mattress. Using his knees, he spread her legs apart and positioned himself between them. Like a heat-guided missile, he found her core without difficulty.

Vivian's lips parted, but no words escaped. Delivering a powerful stroke, she sputtered a whimper. While her mouth had felt excellent on him, there was no comparison to how good it felt being inside of her.

He drove several faster, harder strokes, then pulled out of her wetness.

Vivian attempted to protest. "Don't—"

He covered her mouth with his, halting whatever protest she had. Pulling away, he said, "Do you want me back inside of you?"

"Y-yes. R-right now."

He chuckled. "There's no rush, baby. We have all night. Just lie back and let me love on you."

"I—I want you to love *in* me."

Alonso peppered kisses to her collarbone, causing Vivian to shiver under him. Inching farther down her torso, he glided his tongue over one of her taut nipples, then sucked it into his mouth. His tongue twirled, flicked, lapped before moving to the opposite breast and giving it equal attention. Damn, he loved how her body responded to him.

Venturing lower, he placed a tender kiss to her belly button. At the warmth between her thighs, he spread her wide and brushed his stiffened tongue across her clit. Once. Twice. A third time for good measure.

Vivian whined. "*Please*...Alonso."

His tongue glided across her again. "Please, what, baby? Tell me what you want."

"I want...I want you to taste me. Eat me. Devour me."

Well, he believed in giving his woman whatever she wanted. His lips closed around her clit, and he suckled her gently. Vivian's cries filled the room. The beautiful sound only made him more determined. He curled two fingers inside of her and moved them in and out slowly.

When she slapped both hands on the back of his head and ground herself against his mouth, he knew she was close to the edge. A moment later, she erupted, her body bucking and arching off the bed.

Vivian's body still trembled when he entered her again. The feel of her pulsating around him aroused him even more. His swift strokes slapped against her again and again. It wasn't long before he experienced the sensations of his own impending orgasm.

He rested his hands behind Vivian's knees and pinned her legs to her chest. He drove himself in and out of her with speed and force. A sweltering fire burned through his veins and threatened to ignite him. Sweat streamed down his forehead and into his eye, but the sting wasn't enough to deter him. He was too close to the finish line.

Unable to fight it a second longer, the orgasm tore through him. He gripped the wooden headboard to keep from toppling over. Once-sturdy strokes turned clumsy, but he continued until he had nothing more to give.

Alonso collapsed next to Vivian and pulled her into his arms. He loved feeling her naked body against his.

"I can't wait until you open your birthday present," Vivian said. "I think you're going to love what's inside. Blanche thought so, too."

His head jerked forward. "Blanche...from the lingerie shop in Carolina Beach?"

Vivian smirked. "She ships."

An image of the very revealing patterned body stocking with the lace-up back, cupless bra and open crotch played in his mind. It renewed his hunger. "Why wait?" He made a move to get up, but Vivian urged him back down.

"We have all night. Right now, I just want to be held."

How could he argue with that? Silence played between them. This was okay, because there were truly no words that could possibly contend with this moment.

"I love you, Alonso Wright."

Well, he was man enough to admit when he was wrong. And he'd been wrong. There were three words capable of trumping this moment. "I love you, Vivian Moore."

And he was sure he would for the rest of his life.

Chapter 21

Sitting across from Tressa on the patio of the Mediterranean bistro they'd stopped at for lunch, Vivian felt a wave of sympathy for her friend. This should have been the happiest time of her life, but nothing about her impending wedding appeared to be bringing her much joy.

"Everything is going wrong, Vi. The venue for the engagement party overbooked. Guess who got the boot? The invitations to the engagement party are missing in action. I kissed Roth in your kitchen. I haven't made any wedding plans."

Vivian's head jerked as Tressa's nonchalant confession filtered through her brain. "*Whoa, whoa, whoa.* Back up. You did *what* in my kitchen?"

Tressa groaned, then planted her face in her hands. She shook her head as if doing so would alter her reality. Finally facing Vivian again, she said in a whisper, "I kissed Roth. The night we were at your place prepping for Alonso's birthday party."

Vivian remembered the night well. It'd been the night she and Alonso pledged their love to one another. It'd only been a few weeks ago, but it felt like they'd been in love for forever. Pushing the happy thought aside, she gawked at her friend. *"Tress."*

"This is bad, I know. I don't know what happened, Vi. One minute my lips were wrapped around his saxophone, the next they were wrapped around him."

By no means was this a laughable situation, but Vivian had to bite back a chuckle from Tressa's choice of words. When Tressa touched her lips, Vivian had an idea her friend was reliving her lip-lock with Roth. And if the faint smile was any indication, she'd enjoyed it.

Tressa snapped out of her trance. "It only lasted a few seconds. And we both admitted it was a *huge* mistake. Well, I admitted it was a huge mistake. Roth really didn't have a chance to say anything. Luckily, you and Alonso arrived. When Roth and I left your place, I hurried to my vehicle just to avoid having to rehash what'd happened."

"Tress."

"I know, Vi. I'm an awful person. What kind of woman cheats on her fiancé?"

Some would attribute this more to a temporary lapse of good judgment than cheating. Either way you labeled it, it wasn't an ideal situation.

Tressa slumped in her chair and cradled herself in her arms. "I wasn't going to tell you. I just wanted to forget it ever happened. But I've been riddled with guilt. It's not like I slept with Roth." She kneaded the side of her neck. "I have to tell him. I have to tell Cyrus I kissed another man."

Vivian was all for truth and honesty in a relationship, but she wasn't sure it was necessary to rock the boat over a kiss that had only lasted a few seconds. Unless… *Nah.* Could it be possible? Could Tressa hope by telling Cyrus he would call off the wedding? Was Tressa having second thoughts?

Tressa speared a forkful of salad, then allowed the utensil to drop into the bowl. "I don't know what to do. I feel like I'm damned if I do and damned if I don't."

Vivian reached across the table and took Tressa's hand into hers, giving it a reassuring squeeze. "You and Cyrus seem happy together, Tress, but are you sure you're ready to commit your life to him? If you're having second thoughts…"

Vivian started to insert the short time they'd known each other, but considered her own situation. She'd known Alonso less time than Tressa had known Cyrus and she was head over heels in love with Alonso.

Hell, maybe they were both crazy. But hey, wasn't that love? Daring to risk it all.

"He's good to me, Vi. He spoils me rotten. And I know he loves me." Tressa's gaze slid away. "I'm just not…"

"You're just not what, Tress?"

Tressa shook her head. "Nothing. I love him. And I do want to marry him."

Though Tressa flashed a brilliant smile, Vivian wasn't wholly convinced happiness was what her friend truly felt. She would support Tressa in any decision she made. She just hoped her friend was making the right one. In love, there weren't supposed to be doubts.

Alonso rested his elbows on his desk and stared at Roth. It'd been a long time since he'd seen him rattled. Hell, now that he thought about it, he wasn't sure he'd ever really seen the man frazzled. The troubled man sitting across from him in his office was in stark contrast to the stern man Roth normally displayed to the world.

"I know, man. I know. You don't even have to say it. It was stupid and foul as hell." Roth pushed to his feet and paced back and forth. "But I couldn't resist. When her mouth touched mine, it was a done deal." He sighed heavily.

Alonso definitely understood temptation. He recalled how hard it'd been resisting Vivian before they became an item.

Roth scrubbed a hand over his head. "Enough about me and my bullshit." Roth dropped back into the chair again and grinned. "Should I be getting fitted for a tux, or what?"

Alonso barked a laugh. "Why in the hell do you and Ham keep trying to marry me off?"

"Probably because we both see where this is leading." Roth's expression turned serious. "On the real, bro, I like Vivian. She's good for you. I don't think I've ever seen you this happy."

That would be because he'd never been this happy. He massaged his cheek. "She threw me a birthday party, man. I still can't get over that. Do you know how much that meant to me?" Yeah, it would probably seem insignificant to some, but she'd given him something he'd never had. "Thank you again for helping her out."

"Anything for you, bro. You know that."

Alonso's desk phone beeped, then his assistant's voice boomed over the line. "Pardon the interruption, Mr. Wright, but Garth Garrison is on the line for you again."

Alonso's face hardened. "Take a message, Jessica. Tell him I'm in an all-day meeting."

"Yes, sir."

"Uh-oh. Trouble in paradise?" Roth said.

Alonso hadn't shared with Roth how Garth had gone ballistic in his office and how he'd had to jack him up. He washed his hand down his face. "He wasn't too keen on the idea of me changing the plans for the downtown Raleigh project. Money truly is the root of all evil."

Roth leaned forward and rested his elbows on his thighs.

"I imagine that weasel is trying to secure every dime he can get. Word on the street is he's got some serious gambling debt."

"Huh." Now it made sense why Garth was so pissed by the decrease in revenue. "What's up between you two? You clearly have never liked the man."

"He and his boys came to the club once and were disrespectful to a few of the female staff."

"You never told me that."

"I knew you two had a working relationship."

When Roth stood and moved to the table display, Alonso joined him.

"I love what you've decided to do in the community. Vivian really is a good influence on you."

"The love of a good woman…it changes you." And he was truly a changed man.

Chapter 22

Vivian made haste down the brightly lit corridor. At eight in the evening on a Wednesday, the ER should have been calm—or at least calmer than it had been the past couple of hours. Unfortunately, every time it rained, automobile accidents kept them moving nonstop.

"Pediatric trauma. ETA, ten minutes. Pediatric trauma. ETA, ten minutes."

Vivian always hated when that particular indicator blared over the PA system. Pediatric traumas always rattled her. You never knew what you would see; you just knew that nine times out of ten, it would be bad.

Two hours later, Vivian stumbled into the nurses' lounge and dropped onto one of the leather lounge chairs. She eyed the Keurig machine sitting on the counter. She could really use a cup of coffee but couldn't will her body to make the short trek across the room to get it.

If her feet could talk, she was sure they'd praise her for giving them mercy. On second thought, they'd probably blast her for not giving them a reprieve sooner. Where was Alonso when she needed him? He gave the best foot rubs.

Alonso. The thought of him mimicked a calming elixir. He'd been so concerned when they'd briefly spoken. Especially when she'd broken down crying as she told him about the toddler they'd lost. It hadn't been the first child they'd lost in the ER, but something about this one got to her.

Maybe it'd been the god-awful sound of grief the child's father had released when he'd been given the devastating news that he'd lost his only child.

We were going to get ice cream, he'd repeated several times.

The words were stuck in her head.

"Vi, you in here?"

"No, there's no Vi here," she said in response to Tressa's query.

"Ha-ha. Very funny." Tressa took her arm and coaxed her off the chaise. "I need you to come with me."

Vivian whined. "*Tress.* No. I just want to relax, possibly eat, and consume several cups of coffee."

Tressa ignored her and shepherded Vivian's weary body to the door. They moved down the hall, coming to a stop in front of one of the several patient consultation rooms on the floor. Tressa directed Vivian inside. Instead of Tressa joining her, she closed the door leaving Vivian standing alone in the small vestibule that led into the sitting area.

"Tressa—"

When someone cleared their throat, Vivian rotated. She gasped. "Alonso?" Her brow furrowed. "What are you doing here?"

He held out his hand and she moved toward him. The sight before her garnered a huge smile. Several Chinese take-out containers sat atop the wooden table. The delicious aromas wafting in the room made her stomach growl.

This was just what she needed: food and quiet time with her man.

Vivian looked up at him with adoring eyes. "Thank you."

"You're welcome."

He kissed her gently. She'd missed the feel of his lips against hers. She moaned when his hands glided down her body and squeezed her ass. After what seemed like an eternity, she broke their connection. "You're going to make it hard for me to return to work."

Alonso glided a bent finger along her cheek. "Well, for the next hour, you don't have to think about work. Nothing but relaxing." He led her to the table, pulled out her chair and guided her down.

Vivian grinned. "You are just full of surprises."

Alonso eased into the seat across from her. "You're not the only one with a few tricks up their sleeve."

After enjoying their meal, Vivian and Alonso moved to the two-person couch. He lifted her legs into his lap, removed her black clogs and kneaded her feet.

"*Mmm.* You don't know how great that feels."

"Judging by the moan, I would say pretty spectacular."

"Thank you for all of this. You've made my night. But it's late. *And* I thought you were prepping for the huge meeting you have in the morning?"

"Everything stops when you need me. And I got the impression you needed me. You do need me, right?"

"Absolutely." Admitting that should have been a lot scarier than it actually was. She was making beautiful progress.

Alonso winked at her. "Good."

"Do you want kids, Alonso?" The question had come completely out of left field, and she wasn't sure why she'd even asked it. Maybe because of the father she'd sympathized with earlier or maybe out of sheer curiosity.

Alonso paused and eyed her. "No."

Though the response bothered her—mainly because she did want kids, a house full of them—he'd been honest and she respected that.

Alonso returned his attention back to her feet. "At least not until I find the one. The one I'm so in love with that I would show up at her job at a ridiculous hour, in the pouring rain, with Chinese takeout. When I find that woman, with her I want everything—kids, white picket fences, dogs. With her I want it all, including forever."

Alonso never looked at her; he simply kept his eyes on her feet. Was he afraid of what he would see? Did he believe his words would unnerve her? If so, he was wrong. If anything, they'd done the complete opposite. Instead of unsettling her, they empowered her. Hadn't he just told her he intended to spend his life with her and that he did indeed want children?

"I love you, Alonso P. Wright."

This drew his attention to her. "Never stop. Doing it or saying it."

"Trust me, I won't."

The hour sailed by. Vivian said a reluctant goodbye to Alonso and she returned to the floor. Several eternities later, the clock finally struck 8:00 a.m. Thursday morning, making Vivian a free woman.

Unfortunately, before she could make her clean getaway, Gemma called out to her. Vivian loved Gemma like a sister, but she refused to work one more minute. Her bed was calling her name. Turning, Vivian had to smile at the very pregnant woman wobbling toward her. Though Gemma was only five months, it looked as if she would pop any second.

Gemma pushed a large caramel-colored envelope toward Vivian. "Someone left this for you."

Vivian's nose crinkled. "For me?"

"Yes."

"Huh." Accepting the envelope, she tucked it under her arm, deciding not to open it until she got to her vehicle. "Thank you and I'll see you tonight." Vivian rested her hand on Gemma's protruding belly. "Take it easy, momma."

Gemma saluted her. "Yes, ma'am."

Outside, Vivian pulled in a lungful of the crisp and humid air. Luckily, it'd stopped raining. Hopefully it would hold off until she made the drive home. She disliked driving in the rain.

The scent of something delicious—and artery clogging— invaded her nostrils. Whatever it was, she wanted some. The Chinese food Alonso had brought the night before had long been worked off.

"Need a ride to your vehicle, Ms. Vivian?"

Vivian turned toward the familiar voice. Ronnie, one of Tender Hearts's several security personnel, rolled up on his golf cart. If someone were truly in danger, she wasn't sure how much help Ronnie would be. He was in his early sixties and round as a parade float. But what he lacked in physical appearance, he made up for in sparkling personality. He was one of the most kindhearted people she'd ever met.

Vivian fixed her mouth to decline the ride, but reconsidered. "Sure."

They made small talk as they ventured toward the fifth level of the parking deck. At the speed Ronnie drove, Vivian was sure she could have gotten to her car faster on foot. Finally reaching their destination, she thanked Ronnie for the ride. He sat until she slid safely behind the wheel and cranked the engine.

When she tossed up her hand, he drove away. Instead of backing out of her space, Vivian tore into the envelope she'd been given. Her eyes slowly scanned the document addressed to Raleigh's Housing and Building Standards, Code Enforcement Division.

Noting the signature scribed at the bottom of the damning letter—Alonso P. Wright—her stomach churned and bile coated the back of her throat. She shook her head in disbelief. "No." She wanted to believe this was some kind of forgery, but there was no mistaking the distinct mark.

Alonso downed his third cup of French vanilla–flavored coffee. He wasn't sure how, but Vivian had converted him into a java drinker. Now he couldn't get enough of the stuff. To say he was tired would have been an understatement. It'd been eleven when he'd left the hospital the night before and close to midnight before he'd gotten home—courtesy of the sheets of rain and reckless drivers. Then he'd gone over his presentation one last time, because he needed it perfect.

It'd been close to two in the morning before he'd crawled into bed. He rotated his head. If he hadn't needed the adrenaline rush, he would have skipped the gym and claimed that extra hour of sleep.

The smile he'd witnessed on Vivian's face made his lack of quality sleep worth it. Damn, he loved that woman and missed her when she wasn't around. Maybe after his meeting, he'd hightail it across town and slide under the covers with her. What better way to spend a rainy Thursday than falling asleep with the woman he loved snuggled in his arms? Yeah, that sounded like one hell of a good plan.

"Mr. Wright, the mayor has just arrived. I've shown him into the conference room."

Alonso glanced at his watch. The mayor was early. He took that as a good sign that the man was eager to hear his presentation. "Thank you, Jessica. Buzz me when the others arrive."

"Will d— *Whoa.*"

Jessica's words alarmed him. "What's wrong?"

"Um… Ms. Moore…"

Before Jessica finished the thought, his office door flung open and Vivian stalked in. The hairdo that had been flawless mere hours earlier was now a mop of soggy curls. The purple scrubs he'd wanted so desperately to rip off her were soaked and clung to her body.

He rounded his desk. "Vi, baby—"

With an outstretched arm, she warned him off. He realized the wetness on her face hadn't come from the rain but from her tears. A feeling of doom consumed him. What the hell was going on?

"On the drive over, I thought about all of the things I would say to you. Tell you how I'd believed you. How I'd trusted you. How I'd allowed myself to love you like I've never loved another man." She shook her head and shrugged. "Standing here, I no longer see the purpose. None of it matters anymore."

"Vivian, tell me what's wrong."

"Mr. Wright?"

"What!" *Shit.* He hadn't meant to yell at Jessica. His confusion had him aggravated. Kneading his now throbbing temple, he calmed his tone. "Yes, Jessica?"

"They're waiting for you in the conference room."

"Let them know I'll be there momentarily."

"Yes, sir."

"Vivian—"

Vivian slung a folder toward him. "If you want my house that bad…" She removed a key from her ring and hurled that at him, too. "It's yours." As she backed away, she said, "Stay away, Alonso. Just…stay away."

Before he could say another word, she bolted from his office. He tore into the envelope and removed the single page inside. His stomach knotted. Rounding his desk, he yanked open his drawer. Of course the letter he'd written so long ago wasn't there, because it was in his hand.

He saw red. Balling the paper in a tight fist, he propped himself against his desk. He clenched his teeth so hard it hurt. *"Garth,"* he said in a growl.

But how in the hell had he gotten the letter out of— He paused, his eyes sliding toward his door. Pressing a button on his phone, he said, "Jessica, may I see you, please?"

Chapter 23

Vivian could feel Tressa's eyes boring into her when she allowed yet another call from Alonso to go unanswered. She refused to acknowledge her friend because, without asking, she knew what Tressa was thinking. That she was being unfair. Of course Tressa would never tell her that, because the woman was the epitome of support.

Rocking in the chair on Tressa's porch, Vivian closed her eyes and enjoyed the warm breeze brushing across her face.

"Vi," Tressa said gently, "you can't keep ignoring him. You two need to talk. Give him an opportunity to explain. He deserves that much."

He deserved nothing. And she didn't want to talk to him. She'd said everything she'd needed to say three days ago in his office. As far as she was concerned, there was nothing else left to talk about or explain. He'd deceived her. How could he explain that away?

Still, the pain she felt was real. He'd lied to her from

the beginning. The idea of him being the one responsible for the city coming down on her made the hurt that much worse. She'd spent thousands she didn't have, because of the man who'd claimed to love her.

Vivian's eyes opened slowly, a stray tear escaping from the corner. "He looked me dead in my eyes and lied to me, Tressa."

Granted, they had been nothing more than strangers at the time she'd confronted him about the letter from the city she'd received. Now they were so much more. She scolded herself. How had she allowed herself to fall in love with a man capable of being so devious?

"I blame myself. I should have known he was lying. He's a man and his lips were moving. Why would I believe anything he had to say now? How could he do this to me, Tressa? I... I thought he loved me," she said in a whisper.

"Vivian, he didn't know you then. Not like he knows you now. Several months ago you were just business. Now you're everything to him. Anyone can see that. Just observing the way he looks at you melts my heart. He does love you, Vi. Deep down you know this."

All she knew was that she was angry as hell. At herself. At Alonso. At love in general. "He's had hundreds of opportunities to come clean, but he chose not to."

"And if he had? What would you have done?"

Vivian blew a heavy breath. She didn't know. But if he'd just been honest with her, maybe she could have forgiven him. Instead, he'd continued to perpetrate the lie. Every moment she'd spent with him had been based on a lie.

"He was afraid of losing you, Vi. In his shoes, I might have done the same thing." Her voice lowered. "Hell, I am doing the same thing."

Vivian knew Tressa was referring to her not telling her fiancé about kissing Roth.

Tressa continued, "You might have done the same thing.

No one wants to lose the person they love. Have you even considered why someone would deliver you a copy of that letter? It's obvious they wanted to sabotage your relationship."

Yes, she had. But why? Why would anyone want— A face appeared in her head.

"Vi? What's wrong?"

"The last time we were at The Underground, Alonso introduced me to someone he used to do business with. It was obvious there was some tension between the two of them. He'd given me a bad feeling."

"Would he have had access to the letter?"

Vivian shrugged. "I don't know. I guess. I don't know." Vivian massaged her throbbing temple. "It doesn't matter how the letter got to me. It got to me. And it was Alonso's signature on it. No one else's."

Tressa sat forward in her chair. "I'm just going to say it, Vi. That stupid letter is irrelevant. You have doubt. Understandable. And if that doubt is stronger than your love for Alonso, then hell, maybe you should move on. But I know you love him, too. And I also think you're overreacting."

Vivian's lips parted to say something, but she reconsidered her words. Instead, she reclined her head back again and closed her eyes. She didn't have enough energy for another battle in her life. No one could tell her how she should react because no one knew the courage it had taken for her to love Alonso.

Alonso tried to tune out the chatter going on around him inside Hamilton's place. He didn't give a damn what Roth or Hamilton had to say, he was mad as hell. And he had the right to be. For days, he'd tried to plead his case to Vivian, but she'd shut him out of her life as if he hadn't meant shit to her.

He sprang forward, resting his elbows on his legs. Damn

right he was pissed. And if she no longer wanted anything to do with him, that was fine and all right with him. A minute later, he slumped back into the sofa cushion. Who the hell was he kidding? He was miserable without her.

"You should try calling her again," Roth said.

"No."

Roth made a disapproving sound. "So that's it? You're just going to let her slip away?"

"Yep."

Hamilton placed what looked like spinach artichoke dip on the table in front of them. "You gon' let that damn stubbornness make you lose the best thing that's ever happened to you."

Alonso groaned and allowed his head to fall back against the cushion. "Are we here to celebrate or discuss my messed-up love life?"

Though he had gone into the meeting with the city officials half off his game, he'd been able to convince everyone in the room that supporting his project was a win-win for them all and especially for the community. And when he'd tossed in the publicity angle, they'd supported his initiative wholeheartedly.

The win should have made him extremely happy, but he didn't have the woman he loved to share the triumph with. Plus, she'd been the driving factor behind the project.

"You know I love you, man, but I gotta put this out there. You're a damn idiot." Roth half laughed, half sighed. "Do you know how blessed you are? You've found the woman of your dreams—your words, not mine—and you're not going to fight for her?"

"Y'all are making me out to be the bad guy here. Are you forgetting that she claimed to love me yet believed I was capable of sending that letter?"

"*Ta-hee-hee.* Boy, are you forgetting that you *were* capable of sending it? Didn't you tell us you wrote the letter?"

Yeah, he had. Alonso hung his head, a wave of brutal shame washing over him. "That was the old me. The new me would never hurt anyone like that. Especially her."

Roth clapped Alonso on the shoulder. "That's the Alonso she needs to see. The one who would never hurt her. That's the one she fell in love with."

"Yeah, well, how do I show her that man when I can't even get her to look at me?"

Hamilton laughed. "*Ta-hee-hee.* I think I can help with that."

Chapter 24

Vivian was a mess. She wasn't sure how she'd managed to hold it together, but she had. Maybe because she'd immersed herself in work. Staying busy was supposed to keep her mind off Alonso. Much good it did.

Even though it'd been a week since the last time he'd reached out to her, she thought about him every waking moment and dreamed about him every sleeping one. That, of course, was when she slept.

She slammed her hand against the cold metal of her locker, tears clouding her eyes. All she wanted to do was forget him. Why couldn't she forget him? Forget him as swiftly as he'd shattered her heart.

"Ms. Moore."

Vivian jerked at the sound of Ms. Kasetta's arid tone and swiped at her eyes. All she needed was for the woman to think she couldn't perform her job effectively, which at the moment might have been true. Without making eye contact, she said, "Morning, Ms. Kasetta." She shifted the opposite direction and moved toward the exit with her head low.

"You're a rare breed, Ms. Moore."

Vivian stopped shy of the door. What did that mean?

"I see you. Doing things others won't do. Volunteering before even being asked. Eagerly assisting your coworkers. Treating patients like family."

Vivian slowly rotated toward her. As always, the woman stood straight as a brick wall, stone-faced, her hands cupped behind her back. Vivian had no idea how to respond, because she had no idea where the conversation was headed. "Thank you." *I think.*

"I see a lot. Which is how I know something is off with you."

Obviously Vivian hadn't done as good of a job as she'd thought of keeping her personal and professional lives separate. Who was she kidding? Of course she hadn't. She was in the damn lounge crying over a man.

Ms. Kasetta continued, "I don't know what is going on—"

"I'm just—"

"—and I'm not sure I need to know."

Vivian clammed up like a child who'd just been given "that look" by a parent. She imagined the proverbial look Ms. Kasetta had given her translated to: *get it together.* When Ms. Kasetta ambled past her and out the room, Vivian released the breath she'd been strangling.

When her cell phone rang inside her locker, she jolted. She'd meant to put it on vibrate, but just like everything else lately, she'd dropped the ball on that, too. By the time she'd gotten to the device, she'd missed the call. Checking the caller ID revealed it'd been Hamilton.

Despite what had happen between her and Alonso, she liked Hamilton a lot and would continue to do anything she could to help him. Pressing the callback button, she waited for Hamilton's jolly voice to dance over the line.

"Hello?"

"Hamilton? It's Vivian. I just missed your call. Is everything okay?"

"*Ta-hee-hee.* Everything's fine, pretty lady. Just can't get this darn machine to come on. I know how important you said it is to check my numbers, but this doggone contraption won't strike a lick. I know you're busy and all, but I was sho' hoping you could swing by and take a look at it sometime."

Vivian laughed to herself. The last time Hamilton couldn't get his glucose meter to work, the drum of test strips had been empty. The next time, he'd put the batteries in backward. She wondered what would be the issue this go-round. "Anything for you. I can be there around seven this evening. Is that okay?"

"Fine. Just fine. I sho' do appreciate you and I'll see you at seven."

Ending the call with Hamilton, Vivian took a deep breath. It was time she got her head back in the game and forced Alonso Wright out of her system.

Alonso didn't like the idea of ambushing Vivian, despite how badly he wanted to see her. When she got to Hamilton's place tonight and saw him there, he was sure she would go ballistic. If she'd wanted to see him, she would have taken one of his numerous calls.

Hamilton's words rang in his ears: *sometimes we need to be pushed in the right direction.* Alonso was sure Vivian wouldn't think moving toward him was the right direction. She seemed determined to get as far away from him as she could.

He just needed her to listen. A courtesy she'd denied him. After tonight, if she still wanted nothing to do with him, he would respect that. As difficult as it would be, he would let her go.

The thought knotted his stomach. He lifted the picture of her from his desk and stared at it. If he could only go back in time. Her absence had been pure hell. He hadn't been able to manage a week without her. How in the hell would he manage forever?

"You changed me, woman," he said, then returned the frame back to his desk.

Changed him for the better, which was why he hadn't retaliated against Garth. He'd been poised to ruin the man. And he could have with one call. But Vivian's sweet voice had floated into his head: *we were put here to help people, not hurt them.* Garth would never know this, but he owed Vivian…everything.

Two hours later, he stood face-to-face with a confused Vivian in Hamilton's living room. He'd expected her to turn on her heels and flee once she saw him, but so far, that hadn't happened. He took it as a good sign.

His lips parted, but no words escaped. The only thing he could process was how beautiful she was and how much he'd missed her. Obviously she'd come there straight from work because she was still wearing hot-pink scrubs.

The tips of his fingers tingled. All he wanted to do was reach out and touch her. Twirl one of her bouncy curls around his finger like he did when she was snuggled in his arms. So many beautiful moments flooded him that his chest tightened as if he were drowning in the memories.

"Where's Hamilton?" she asked.

Vivian's words pulled him back to reality. "Ah, he's not here." Instantly, her demeanor shifted. Alonso assumed it'd dawned on her that she'd been set up. "Don't blame Ham."

"I don't." She turned to leave.

"Take a ride with me." His words clearly stunned Vivian, because she stopped so abruptly he thought she'd topple over.

Facing him, she said, "Why would I do that?"

"Please, Vivian." Her expression softened a hint and it gave him minimal hope. "Please."

Vivian rolled her eyes away. "Where?"

"I can't tell you."

Her eyes darted back to him. "Why?"

"Because I need to show you."

Her gaze drifted away again. He could tell she was mulling over his request. A beat later, she nodded. It was a small victory, but a victory nonetheless.

Chapter 25

The drive to wherever they were headed was a quiet one. Vivian refused to even look at Alonso, let alone hold a conversation with him. When she'd walked into Hamilton's place and seen him standing there in his tailored dark business suit, it'd taken her breath away. How could his presence still be so powerful?

As much as she wanted to ignore him, her body continued to respond to him. His nearness, his scent, his beautiful build. She hated herself right now. For lusting for him. For still loving him. For getting in this vehicle with him headed to only God knew where.

Why was she so weak when it came to lying Alonso? The silly name garnered a laugh she'd intended to hold inside.

"What's funny?" he asked.

Vivian sobered. Sliding her gaze from the windshield, she settled it out of the passenger side window. "Nothing," she said drily.

So lost in her thoughts, Vivian hadn't noticed the route they'd taken until they turned onto the street she'd grown up on. When her childhood home came into view, she shot a glance in Alonso's direction. "What are we doing here?"

Alonso pulled into her driveway, popped the gearshift into Park and killed the engine. He stared straight ahead. "Everything has a price, Vivian."

Not this again. She'd agreed to deed the house to him. What more could he want?

"Even love." He leveled his gaze on her. "I know this because I'm paying dearly."

Instead of elaborating, he flashed a low-wattage smile and exited the vehicle. When he opened her door, there was a brief moment when she thought he would lean in and kiss her. She was glad he didn't, because she wasn't sure she would have had enough willpower to resist.

Using the key she'd hurled at him in his office, Alonso popped the lock to the front door, then stepped aside to allow her to enter ahead of him. "You still haven't told—" Vivian paused, the setup in the room halting her words. Several easels were placed throughout the living room, all displaying different architectural designs. "What is this?"

"Your vision made reality," Alonso said from behind her.

"My—" Again, she ended midthought. Something special caught her eye. Her grandmother's name in block lettering on one of the display boards. The tip of her finger outlined the letters.

"That's the clinic."

"The clinic?" she said absently.

Alonso moved to each of the displays, labeling as he went. "Community-slash-recreation center. A job-skills facility. Day care center. And, of course, transitional housing. The city has agreed to absorb some of the maintenance cost. And Ham has agreed to be the on-site maintenance man." He chuckled. "He said it'll give him something to do, other than cooking. This is your dream, Vivian. I just wanted to make it come true."

Vivian's head spun. Was he saying he'd done all of this for her? "You altered your plans…for me?"

"Woman, I'll alter my life for you. That's how much I love you."

Vivian folded her arms across her chest and studied her feet. If she held on to his penetrating eyes a second longer, she'd go insane. Batting back the emotions swelling inside of her, she reminded herself of the circumstances that had gotten them here.

"I get why you're upset with me, Vivian. I do. Even though I never sent that letter, at one point, yes, I'd considered it."

The admission forced her to meet Alonso's eyes again. "And that's what hurts so much, Alonso. I have no idea who I fell in love with. I don't know…I don't know the man capable of doing something so low to get what he wants. And I don't want to know him."

"And you never will. The man who signed that paper and *stuffed it in a drawer*," he emphasized, "and the man standing before you now are two completely different people, Vivian."

"How, when they both encompass the same body?"

"The man who signed that letter wanted to be the big man. This man…" He rested an open hand over his chest. "All this man wants to be is a better man. That's what you do for me, Vivian. You make me want to be better, do better. I admit that I haven't always been on the up-and-up with you, but I swear to you I am now."

Rarely did words convince her of anything, but looking into Alonso's eyes, she could feel his sincerity. It chipped away at her doubt.

"I've never known a woman like you, Vivian. And I

can't give you up." He took a step toward her. "Baby, I can't give you up. I could exist without you, but you've gotten me too damn used to actually living. And *that*, I can't do without you."

Vivian swallowed the painful lump stuck in her throat, trapping her words.

"All I want is for you to hear me, Vivian. Feel me. Love me, because I love the hell out of you. I'll give you time, and I'll respect whatever decision you make. And whether you choose me or not, it doesn't change any of this." He swept his hand across the designs. "This will happen regardless."

Vivian bit at the corner of her lip. She fought the tears threatening to spill from her eyes. Emotion—raw, intense, necessary—raged inside of her.

"Come on. I'll take you back to your car."

Vivian rotated toward the displays. Never in her wildest dreams could she have ever imagined a gesture this grand. Never in her wildest dreams would she ever have imagined anyone sacrificing so much for her. "I stood in this room once and asked my grandmother why my parents no longer loved me." Her voice cracked as she forced herself to continue. "In my mind, they'd simply given me away."

Alonso's footsteps shuffled over the floor. Without turning, she could sense him inches from her. And when he finally rested his large hands on her waist and guided her trembling body back against his, she didn't pull away.

"My grandmother told me that one day I'd understand that sacrifice is the purest form of love. I understand that now." The impact of each one of his unbridled words had settled past her heart and into her soul.

"I hear you, Alonso."

Loud and clear.

"I feel you."

Raw and potent.

"And I love you."

Loved him in a manner that defied theory or explanation. Loved him blindly and with full sight.

She wanted his love. *Needed* his love. Refused to continue another second denying it.

Turning, she said, "Are you still in the market for love? Namely, mine?"

Alonso slid his hand up the back of her neck and intertwined his fingers in her hair. With a fistful of her locks, he eased her head back, then smashed his mouth to hers. The intensity of the kiss overwhelmed her. And when her knees buckled, Alonso was there to keep her body from collapsing to the floor.

He kissed her long. He kissed her hard. He satisfied the hunger that had lurked inside of her since they'd been apart.

Breaking their intimate bond, Alonso stared into her eyes. "I love you in so many ways. Don't ever take your love away from me again, woman."

"I won't."

His mouth found hers again, and he kissed her as if it were the very first time their lips had ever touched. Standing there, she knew one thing for certain. She knew she would forever be his. And she had an idea he knew it, too.

Epilogue

Vivian eyed the large diamond on her finger and smiled with the same brilliance she had when Alonso slid it onto her finger two weeks ago. She'd wanted to wait until after Tressa's nuptials to wed, but Alonso had been adamant about making her his wife. So they'd had a small ceremony at dusk on Infinity Island.

"I love watching the sunrise with you, *Mrs. Wright*," Alonso said, tightening his protective arms around her.

Vivian thought back to when they'd first met, when Alonso couldn't stop calling her Mrs. Wright. In a million years, she never would have guessed he'd been foreshadowing their future. "The feeling is mutual, Mr. Wright."

"Are you sure you're not upset that we had to postpone the honeymoon?"

Vivian laughed. "For the thousandth time, no. It was my idea, remember? You have so much going on with the downtown project. I would have felt guilty dragging you away."

"Everything stops for you. You know that."

The words warmed her heart. "We have forever to go on our honeymoon."

"Forever sounds good to me." In a swift move, he had her back on the blanket. "I never dreamed I could ever love anyone as much as I love you, Vivian Wright. Not even myself. I'm proud to call you my wife."

Vivian cradled her husband's face between her hands, tears clouding her vision. She wanted to tell him that she knew exactly how he felt, but was unable to speak past the lump lodged in her throat. Instead, she pulled his mouth to her and kissed him with all the love she held for him.

After what felt like an eternity, Alonso broke their connection. "We're going to have an amazing life together."

She couldn't agree more.

* * * * *

SPECIAL EXCERPT FROM

*After scoring phenomenal success in Phoenix with
her organic food co-op, Naomi Stallion is ready to
introduce Vitally Vegan to her Utah town. But a nasty
bidding war over the property Naomi wants to buy
pits the unconventional lifestyle coach against sexy,
überconservative corporate attorney Patrick O'Brien.
When the stakes rise, will Patrick choose his career or the
woman he yearns for?*

Read on for a sneak peek at
SWEET STALLION,
the next exciting installment in author
Deborah Fletcher Mello's **THE STALLIONS** *series!*

Naomi shifted her gaze back to the stranger's, her palm
sliding against his as he shook her hand. The touch was
like silk gliding across her flesh, and she mused that he had
probably never done a day's worth of hard labor in his life.
"It's nice to meet you, Patrick," she answered. "How can
we help you?"

"I heard you mention the property next door. Do you
mind sharing what you know about it?"

She looked him up and down, her mind's eye assembling
a photographic journal for her to muse over later. His eyes
were hazel, the rich shade flecked with hints of gold and
green. He was tall and solid, his broad chest and thick arms
pulling the fabric of his shirt taut. His jeans fit comfortably

against a very high and round behind, and he had big feet. Very big feet in expensive, steel-toed work boots. He exuded sex appeal like a beacon. She hadn't missed the looks he was getting from the few women around them, one of whom was openly staring at him as they stood there chatting.

"What would you like to know about Norris Farms?" Naomi asked. She crossed her arms over her chest, the gesture drawing attention to the curve of her cleavage.

Patrick's smile widened. "Norris," he repeated. "That's an interesting name. Is it a fully functioning farm?"

"It is. They use ecologically based production systems to produce their foods and fibers. They are certified organic."

"Is there a homestead?"

"There is."

"Have the owners had it long? Is there any family history attached to it?"

Naomi hesitated for a brief second. "May I ask why you're so interested? Are you thinking about bidding on this property?"

Patrick clasped his hands behind his back and widened his stance a bit. "I'm actually an attorney. I represent the Perry Group and they're interested in acquiring this lot."

Both Naomi and Noah bristled slightly, exchanging a quick look.

Naomi scoffed, apparent attitude evident in her voice. "The Perry Group?"

Patrick nodded. "Yes. They're a locally owned investment company. Very well established, aren't they?"

Her eyes narrowed as she snapped, "We know who they are."

Don't miss SWEET STALLION
by Deborah Fletcher Mello, available September 2017
wherever Harlequin® Kimani Romance™
books and ebooks are sold!

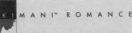

Get 2 Free Books,
Plus 2 Free Gifts—
just for trying the Reader Service!

KROM17R2

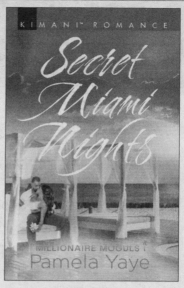

Reward the book lover in you!

Earn points from all your Harlequin book purchases from wherever you shop.

Turn your points into *FREE BOOKS* of your choice
OR
EXCLUSIVE GIFTS from your favorite authors or series.

Join for FREE today at
www.HarlequinMyRewards.com.

Harlequin My Rewards is a free program (no fees) without any commitments or obligations.

MYR17